Walking with Ghosts

New Prose & Poetry from Perthshire & Beyond

Alan J. Laing

"Walking With Ghosts – New Prose & Poetry from Perthshire & Beyond"
Copyright © Alan J. Laing 2017. All rights reserved.

The right of Alan J. Laing to be identified as the author
of the Work has been asserted by him in accordance with the
Copyright, Designs & Patents Act 1988.
This edition published and copyright 2017 by
Tippermuir Books Ltd, Perth, Scotland.
mail@tippermuirbooks.co.uk
www.tippermuirbooks.co.uk

The publisher is not responsible for websites (or their content)
that are not owned by the publisher. No part of this publication
may be reproduced or used in any form or by any means without
written permission from the Publisher except for review purposes.
All rights whatsoever in this book are strictly reserved.
All characters and events in this publication, other than those
clearly in the public domain, are fictitious and any resemblance
to real persons, living or dead, is purely coincidental.

ISBN: 978-0-9954623-3-5 (paperback)
A CIP catalogue record for this book is available
from the British Library.

Text styling and layout:
Bernard Chandler [graffik], Glastonbury, England.

Production Support:
Ajay Close, Jean Hands, Matthew Mackie, and Steve Zajda
Illustrations: Robert A. Hands
Cover design: Robert A. Hands and Matthew Mackie
Editorial and Project Management: Dr Paul S. Philippou

Text set in 11/16pt Sabon, with
11.5pt Baskerville Italic and Caflisch Script Pro

Printed and bound by CPI Group (UK) Ltd, Croydon CR0 4YY.

For Maisie, who always kept me on the right path.

ACKNOWLEDGEMENTS

My thanks go to many people who have contributed to the production of this book. First of all to two of the Tippermuir team, Paul and Matthew, for their highly professional work in editing and cover design, and to Bernard for the book layout and typography. Paul's editing expertise has taught me how much more there is to a book than just writing some stories.

A special thanks to Rob, the other Tippermuir team-member, and the provider of the cover painting, illustrations, maps and cartoons which give the texts such added life. For most of the settings I had a clear picture in my mind, having walked or climbed there. Transferring those visual pictures into the minds of readers would have been a task beyond me without Rob's cartographic and artistic abilities.

Thanks also go to the various people who read my first stories and encouraged me to write more. In particular 'Mountaineering Scotland', whose 'Mountain Writing' competitions convinced me that my writing could be appreciated by objective judges.

And finally, to all the folk I have walked and climbed with over the years, above all the guys of The Three Times a Year Club, for whom hill-walking is important, but never ever serious.

⁜

CONTENTS

Foreword

Introduction

THE LAST CALL-OUT	1
GEOMETRY	7
GLENCOE.CO.UK	9
LAND OF THE MOUNTAIN AND THE FLOOD	15
MACBETHADMACWHO?	19
NEAR SHINIGAG	28
FAIR CITY FRIENDS	29
PERTH 2040	40
IN YOUR PLACE	49
MORNING WALK	50
DEATH AND LIFE IN THE MOUNTAIN	51
THE GOOD COMPANION	58
ALIEN IN ETIVE	65
YOU'LL NEVER WALK ALONE	73
THE PALE MOUNTAINS	74
SIDEWALK RAGE	83
'THE ICE-MAN'	91
THE CHOOKY	99
SUPERIORITY OF MANKIND	112
THE WALKERS	113
DRAWING TO A HALT	122
TRI UAIREAN'S A'BHLADHNA	124
THE LAST MUNRO	130

FOREWORD

ONE OF THE PERKS of being editor of *Scottish Mountaineer* magazine is the pleasure of publishing the winners in the annual Mountaineering Scotland writing competition. The standard of entries is always high and the standard of the winners higher still.

And Alan Laing has won so often – in both prose and poetry sections – that I've even toyed with the idea of banning him to give others a chance. But then I think how much I enjoy his writing and consign that idea to the bin – where it most assuredly belongs.

Whether it's high drama, flight of fantasy or chuckling comedy, most of Alan's writing relates to mountains and mountaineers, a world where he is completely at home. But his walking is never pedestrian. He's a stravaiger, equally on the mountains and in the less-mapped regions of the imagination. And just as a hill gangrel might spot and follow a faint trod through the glens and into the mountains, he will pick up an idea and see how far it will lead him – or him it.

When Alan merely tells a tale he does so with facility, but so often his stories make use of unusual twists in the route to take the reader to surprise destinations, or use fresh imagery and metaphor to see familiar destinations in new ways.

Making a collection from such a wide-ranging imagination as Alan's is risky: some ideas and their development will seem inspired, while others – for some – might fail to fly. I'll be honest: there are a couple of tales here I might not have chosen, but I won't say which, because they might well be your favourites – and the exploration itself is part of the fun of this book.

Oh. And the poetry? I don't care much for most poetry. But Alan's makes me see things with added depth and colour, makes me think of the mountains in new ways, makes me want to go back to test new truths. I can't ask more than that.

Enjoy.

Neil Reid
Editor, Scottish Mountaineer
(Mountaineering Scotland)

INTRODUCTION

I'M NOT SURE if anyone bothers to read introductions when there are chapters or stories or poems waiting to be read. I even considered putting this one in the middle of the book so that the unwary reader would stumble into it by accident, like an explorer falling into a camouflaged pit. But since you're reading this you're either looking for an insight into the contents of the book before you start reading, or you have read some or all of it and feel the need of some background.

Given the theme of walking, what you're reading now could be likened to a map – though not one as clear and logical as the ones so handsomely provided by illustrator Rob Hands. And if this were indeed a map of what lies ahead you would see that you can be taken, should you wish, to various parts of mountainous Scotland; to the streets of the fine city of Perth – in the past and in the future; to places near Perth – Dunsinane Hill, Quarrymill Woodland Park, and Perth Crematorium; to Glen Etive and Glencoe; to the Italian Dolomites and to the streets of New York. The other setting, for which there is absolutely no map, is the imagination of the author.

What creatures might be found in those cartographic areas? Legend has it that in medieval times uncharted territory was marked, *'Here be dragons'*, and representations would be drawn of dragons and sea-serpents. No dragons will be found here – though you will be taken inside a mountain, the traditional dragon lair. Less frighteningly you will encounter an alien visitor disguised as a mountain hare, a psychotic hamster, a stuffed marmot, and a food-obsessed West Highland Terrier. You'll also meet talking statues, virtual mountains, and an admirable Macbeth. The rest of the characters are straightforward humans: mostly fictional, some historical, some are people I know. There's some poetry too – but there are no maps for poetry. There was of course, a map for the scripted account of the Duke of Edinburgh expedition, *The Chooky*. But I believe the hamster ate it.

Why *Walking with Ghosts*? The 'Walking' part is straightforward. I wrote a couple of stories which involved walking and found that it was a wonderfully flexible context for more – not of the same, but still involving walking of some kind. And why 'with Ghosts'? The book didn't start out that way, and the ghosts don't appear everywhere. But for some reason ghosts of one kind or another appeared quite frequently. I suppose that's what ghosts do – turn up when they want to, not when you ask them to. I think memories can be ghostly too. Sometimes memories which can haunt you; sometimes ones which you wish to stay, to become more substantial, but which just fade away. So then, we have a collection of prose pieces, all of which involve walking of some kind and many of them invoking ghostly presences or memories.

Some of the walking was done by me, more often it was done by characters who walked into my head. Quite often they walked in while I was walking. To all of you out there, carry a small notebook and pencil when you go for a walk. You know all those great ideas and startling insights you get – and then can't remember later? Jot them down. Then write some stories. Or some poems. Or just some thoughts.

Alan J. Laing

The Last Call-out

THE PINE PANELLED ROOM was an Aladdin's Cave, filled not with silks and satin and silver but with kernmantle, Gore-Tex, steel, titanium, fibreglass, carbon fibre. Hard stuff. Sharp, pointy stuff. Beautifully utilitarian things, made for sending you up rocks, along rivers, down snow slopes. The room was what young Sean's Aunt Shena called 'the bourach' and his uncle Martin called his gear room. The accumulation of equipment was testimony to forty years of outdoor activity, twenty years of it in a Mountain Rescue team. In his thirteen years Sean had already done a respectable number of Munros with his Mum and Dad but he knew that Uncle Martin had walked every Munro, climbed in the Alps, canoed in white water, and still skied, as Sean's Dad put it, 'like an avalanche waiting to happen.'

When Sean visited his aunt and uncle in their cottage outside Kingussie he liked to explore this room, taking in the mountain photographs from Scotland and more remote places; picking up and hefting chunky, immensely *practical* looking bits of equipment; imagining himself using those crampons, ice-axes, or the collections of chocks hanging from slings like a jailer's keys. Best of all, if he could persuade his uncle, he liked to hear stories about expeditions or mountain rescues.

"Uncle Martin, what was your best rescue?"

"I don't think I'd say 'best' about any of them, son. Any time we went out it meant someone was in trouble and you never wanted that."

"Even when they were numpties? Even when they didn't have maps and compasses and things?"

"Even them. You hoped they'd learn something from the experience and not need you again."

"Bet you still thought they were numpties though."

"Aye, well, sometimes that thought did cross your mind. But they usually got enough criticism from other folk. I mind one poor guy actually getting slapped by his wife when we brought him in. Then she gave him a big hug."

"So what was the last rescue you did before you left the team?"

"The last call-out? That was a strange one. Maybe the strangest one I ever experienced. Still not sure what to think about it."

"What happened?"

"Ach, you don't want to hear about it."

"Uncle Martin, stop teasing and tell me."

"OK. Just to stop you mithering me. At first it seemed like an ordinary call-out. It was winter time, 1998. Hadn't been a really bad winter but some heavy late snow and strong winds caught out a few folk that maybe hadn't paid enough attention to the forecasts. Sometimes better to have a really bad winter. People know what to expect. Three walkers were reported missing: a father and his two teenage sons, both a bit older than you, Sean. They'd done the right thing – left a note of their route at the hostel they were using, so we knew the rough area they should be in. But by the time they were posted missing it was getting dark and the weather had deteriorated. The snow was heavier and the wind would have been blowing into their faces if they were trying to descend. And what do people do, Sean, when the snow's blowing in your face?"

"They put their heads down."

"And where are they looking?"

"At their boots."

"Exactly. Instead of making sure they're keeping in the right direction. I'm not saying they were doing that, but it's a possibility."

"So where about were they?"

"You know that corrie we went to last year with your Dad? The one with all the mountain hares?"

"Yeah, where Bonnie tried to chase them."

"Right, that was where they had headed to. Safe enough area in good weather but could be tricky in bad visibility. If you didn't find the right way out of that corrie you could end up in some dangerous places. Anyway, we worked out two of the most likely areas where they might be and divided up. I was in a six-man team doing a line-search of the ground they might have got onto if they'd missed the safe route down."

"So you were all in a big line, yeah?"

"Correct. Covering as much ground as possible but still in contact with the guys on either side. Not an easy job on rough terrain. It wasn't quite a whiteout but visibility was down to about ten metres, sometimes less."

'Tiring job walking in line. Physically, and mentally too. Keeping guys in your peripheral vision left and right at the same time as watching the ground in front. Working hard to keep up when your bit of ground had deeper snow, slowing down when easier going tried to push you ahead. Breaking up your normal hill-rhythm. Eyes focused and ears alert. Hoping you would find them but fearing what you might find.'

"And did you find them?"

"Hold on, we'll get to that."

"After about an hour we'd found nothing. We were in radio contact with the other team and they hadn't found anything either. Then Jimmy Robertson – he was on the left-hand end of the line, outside me – he gave me a shout and pointed. I could just make out a figure – hard to tell how far away in these conditions – and he was waving us towards him. Jimmy shouted for him to come across but he didn't seem to hear, just kept waving us in his direction."

'The spindrift narrowing his eyes to defensive slits. The twin head torches, wavering cones, casting the figure in an eldritch light as it turned and moved away. Knowing the danger of the line being broken, so sending a message along to the other guys to mark their stopping point, then follow Jimmy and himself. Keeping the figure in sight but never managing to catch up; stumbling then recalibrating as a hollow camouflaged by banked snow altered his balance; seeing faint patches of darker colour assembling themselves into more solid shapes…then seeing that they were just rocks; looking ahead again for their silent guide…'

"Uncle Martin, why are you stopping? The man was waving. What happened next?"

"Ach, well, he led us on you know, Jimmy and me and the rest of the team. Down into a wee gully right at the edge of the corrie. We wouldn't have known it was there unless we had been looking right down into it. And there they were, in their survival bags, legs in their rucksacks, dug into the bank of the gully."

"Had they not been shouting?"

"They were well past that, Sean. Even stopped shivering."

"Stopped? Is that not good?"

'The bodies were so cold that the brains had stopped sending messages to the nerves to make the muscles contract and relax at speed. They'd stopped creating warmth by expending energy. But breathing, definitely breathing, shallow as it was. Both of them.'

"No, shivering helps heat you up, Sean. Helps stave off some of the 'umbles', you know."

"The what?"

"The 'umbles'. Kind of a shorthand for what happens when you're too cold – *really* too cold. Mumbles, stumbles, tumbles, grumbles, fumbles. Come to think of it, that describes you when you were a wee rugrat."

"Very funny. More like you and Dad after a night in the pub. Now, get back to the story. So you found them?"

"Found two young lads there, but not the father."

"So was that their Dad showing you where they were?"

"That would have seemed logical. Nobody else would have been likely to have been on the mountain at night, in that weather, but our team. He had even been wearing what we'd been told the father had on when he left the hostel. Blue mountain jacket, black hat – and the kind of black overtrousers that most walkers would have put on when it rained or snowed. Jimmy and I both agreed on that. So yes, it looked like it. But he'd disappeared. Like snaw aff a dyke as they say. Which was strange, whoever he was. More than strange."

> 'One moment looking down at the half-buried bodies, then looking up to speak to their strangely uncommunicative guide. Just blackness, a ragged hole cut in it by the beam of the head torch, and sleety, swirling, lunatic parachutes of snow. No human shape. And looking back, two sets of tracks leading towards the following team, tracks already being softened round their edges. Two sets.'

"We got busy on the two lads: checked vital signs, got them talking to us, worked on their core temperatures. Then a message came through from the other team. They had found a body, about two kilometres away. Knew it was the father as he had some identification on him. And a blue jacket, black hat, black overtrousers. And dead. They reckoned he'd tried to walk out for help but collapsed and died before he could make it. If he'd stayed with the boys maybe he would have made it. They were already showing signs of recovery and getting strapped into stretchers so we could evacuate them."

"So who…"

"Who was our guy?"

> 'Back at base, going through the records. Something lodged in the memory. Three or four years back, father and two sons, lost for two days. The boys found dead, father never found, even after the spring thaw. Described as wearing blue jacket, black hat, black overtrousers. Showed the entry to Jimmy, who'd looked at it, then shrugged. Jimmy believed in straightforward stuff: the snowplough turn, accepting what your compass told you, the healing power of whisky. Anything more complex he left others to think about.'

"The guy that led us in? Depends son. Depends what you believe in."

Geometry

On this island of red and black,
Of Gothic pillars and boiler plate slabs,
Sawtoothed tigers and humpbacked whales,
There is a taste for harled boxes
Inside neat rectangular gardens.
They let the landscape know that
Enough is enough.
Behave yourself, they say.
Show a bit of discipline.
When all is gnarled and knotted,
Fractured and fragmented,
When scree inches down
And surf slams in,
We build walls and fences
To try to stop ourselves being crushed,
Or drowned.
There's security in the geometry
of the right angle.

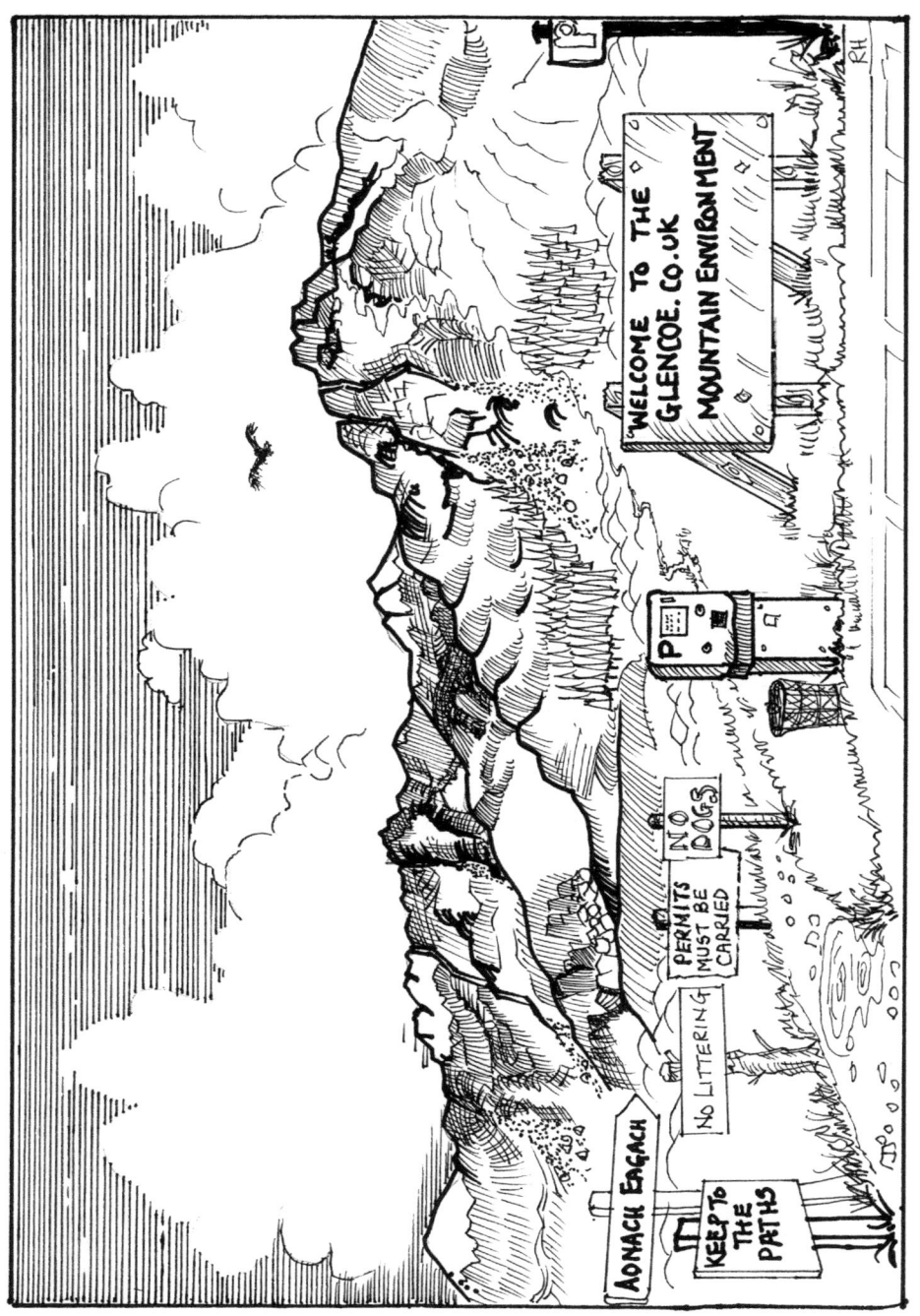

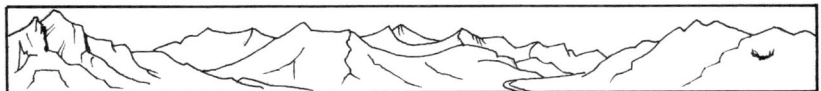

GLENCOE.CO.UK

BUACHAILLE ETIVE MOR floated on a grey duvet of cloud inversion. It back-dropped an LED display-screen endlessly scrolling through its messages:

'Welcome to glencoe.co.uk Mountain Environment. Accommodation capacity currently 748. Climbing Permits and daily or weekly insurance available at Ranger Headquarters first right. Underground Parking 300 metres second right. Buchaille Gondola open 8 a.m. till 6 p.m. Sponsored by Campbell's Organic Steak-House, Glencoe Village Resort.'

Three generations of Grants stood together in the twenty-minute drop-off mini-park and scanned the information. All were bearded: one grizzled, one trim and black, one nearly at the stage of peach-fuzz. The oldest of the three shook his head slowly. The youngest pointed at the Buchaille and asked, "Is that it, the ridge up that left hand side? Is that the Aonach what's-its-name?"

Father and grandfather smiled. Rob Grant, answered the boy.

"No' quite, Adam. You're in the ball park but shootin' at the wrong goals. Turn yersel and take a look back there. The Aonach Eagach. One of the finest ridge walks in Scotland. Me an' your Gran knocked it off summer and winter. Your turn now."

"Jeez. So we're going for a walk along that, Dad?"

Steve Grant, tapping their permit code into his mobile to send their current location to the Rangers' computer, answered without looking up.

"Yup. And you'd better enjoy it. Like I enjoyed it when your Grandad dragged me along in the rain when I was your age."

"Aye – and for free then."

"So, you decided what you're going to do then, Dad? We'll be about five or six hours, if sunshine here gets his backside in gear."

"I told you. I'm goin' to sell my soul again at the VRME centre. Better than nothing, since they've taken away my over-sixty bloody licence – excuse the language Adam. Then I'll get us organised at the motel and maybe have a low-level toddle, if the walk-police allow that."

"Come on Dad, you know what the doctor said. Better safe than sorry. Anyway, see you later at the motel."

"Bye Grandad. No pullin' any loose women now."

"Cheeky wee bugger. He'll come to a bad end." Rob smiled, and turned back to the car.

At the VRME centre Rob slotted in his National ID, typed in the required insurance form information and read the warning messages:

> *'Users must wear appropriate clothing and footwear as temperatures in the VRME chambers will reflect season, altitude and any 'special weather conditions' requested. No food or drink to be taken into the chamber. At designated times energy tablets and hydration drinks will be provided.*
>
> *Do not step off your path simulator while it is moving – if necessary press the 'Rest' or 'Cancel' button on the wrist strap provided.*
>
> *Welcome to the Virtual Reality Munro Environment.'*

Rob clicked 'Read and agreed' and moved on to the route options.

"Schiehallion again? Or maybe Ben Alder – plenty time for that. Or how about Beinn Eighe? Up there twice and never saw much. OK, Beinn Eighe this morning and see if the legs'll take

Alder tomorrow. Christ, that would've been an impressive weekend back then."

He punched in the requisite code, slid in his credit card, pocketed the route card which slid back to him and made his way to the VRME chambers. Checking the number of his chamber he inserted the route card in the slot in the door and as it opened – not with the usual mechanical whirr of such devices but to the sound of a burn over pebbles – he entered. Once inside, arrows on the floor directed him onto a wide, gently-sloping treadmill-style apparatus. In front of him was a screen carrying a further set of options.

Rob hoped his problems with technology wouldn't prove fatal.

"Weather conditions – let's have a nice Autumn day, maybe a bit chilly, but clear to the top. Pace. Don't kid yourself – average. Special options: Wind turbine removal? Nah, used to them now. Eagle sighting, let's have that. Never forget the first time. Music? Are you kiddin' – we're here for the music of nature. Boots on bracken, burn gurglin', and maybe a bit of wheezing. Right let's get on the hill."

He pressed 'Set Off and Enjoy!' With a barely perceptible hum an all-round vision-screen lowered itself over him, stopping inches above the treadmill, which was already transformed by the visualisation graphics into a stony path, and now flanked by heather slopes.

Two figures, one tall and one shorter, moved steadily along the sinuous Aonach Eagach ridge. From below, their progress would have seemed imperceptible, two exotically-coloured insects crawling along a towering grey wall topped by the jagged battlements that were nature's chaotic defence system. To one of the pair the ridge-top was perfectly-designed in degree of difficulty and exposure, neatly balancing challenge and security. To the other it was perfectly-designed to keep him in perpetual doubt about wanting to be there at all. Climbing up, climbing down, climbing round, climbing across; plenty of variety but more or less the same effect for each direction.

The conversation was mostly one-sided and more or less limited to the imperative, the advisory and the sardonic.

"Don't try to go down backwards. Face in."

"There's a big hold up to your left, Adam. That's it. Park a bus on that."

"Get off your knees. They're for praying on. Or is that maybe what you're doing?"

"That's right Dad. I'm praying for some rain now, just to make things really perfect."

Rob gradually felt his legs and body adjust with less and less conscious thought to the ever-changing flexible surface below him as it altered its angle or broke smoothly into wide steps. He'd used the VRME before, on a variety of routes and, despite his initial scepticism, had to marvel at the degree of sophistication involved: the incredible graphics, the blending together of sight, sound and smell into 'A Virtual Outdoor Experience of Stunning Quality'. He'd known that computerisation had moved on since his day – he'd seen some of the games Adam immersed himself in – but was still always surprised at how quickly the suspension of disbelief kicked in.

There was nobody to chat with of course, though you could always hire one of the big multi-chambers as a group. But there was something to be said at his age for the 'intensified experience editing process', which trimmed the route time down to a comfortable couple of hours. You still experienced each significant change of view or terrain, just more briefly. There had been times in the past when that particular facility would have appealed, he supposed, as he and his mates had slogged up a scree, two steps up and one down, or hacked and kicked steps up a hard-crusted snow slope.

The dialogue was even more one-sided, but the tone had softened.

"Keep focusing, Adam. You'll be getting knackered now. That's when accidents happen. You're doing great though. Take a look down there. That's the Clachaig Motel. The ridge stops above it so get down there and I'll maybe buy you a half of Re-energiser."

"A Re-energiser? That'll make this…torture all…worthwhile. And thanks for the rain by the way. Did you order it specially?"

"D'you not remember? You put in an order for it a couple of hours ago. Now you're getting the real Eagach experience. Lucky lad."

Calling up the 'Journey Statistics Screen' with the wrist strap button, and temporarily blocking off part of his view of 'Beinn Eighe', Rob saw that he had progressed half way in twenty-eight minutes, used 300 calories, and his heart-rate was in the 'Safe' category. Clicking back to his 360 degree view he looked over to the quartzite peaks of mighty Liathach and Alligin. He'd always thought the Torridonian mountains the best-presented in Scotland. Laid out like masterpieces in an art gallery. Space between them so you could take them in one by one. And always that feeling that you were looking at some of the oldest lumps of rock in the world.

"Hundreds of millions of years old. There's some the wee human brain just can't take in. And what am I lookin' at? A set of pixels, nano-seconds old and proba feet away. Ach well, better than nothin' I suppose."

From the furthest point of his peripheral vision he s maybe he even sensed it. Before he'd ever seen one he mistaken other large predator birds for it. Once he'd c seen one – and that was only a handful of times in a li he didn't make the mistake again. The golden eagle: lo mountains, monarch of the skies – give it whatever r wanted, it didn't care. If ever there was total self-suffic wings this was it. Rob pressed 'Rest' as the bird floatec The graphics were faultless: every detail of the gold feathers and the russet plumage was sharp and prec beat of the gigantic wings filled his ears.

Rob's mind went back to that first eagle sightir Torridon of his memory. A Torridon he had experien the years in eight hour days of mist, smirr, lashing rain, occasional blazing sunshine. Hard slogging, wonderi you were doing it, then that great series of feelings: the of track; the boots prised off; watching the first pir poured; that sense of...

"Dad! Look up there! There! Is that an eagle?"

Steve paused, one hand anchored to the rock, one his eyes against the watery sun which had finally emerg bird was big right enough, but too far to identify with ac More likely to be a raven, but you did get the occasion sighting in the area. As he turned to Adam he could excitement in the boy's eyes. Was this really the time for a bracing dose of Scottish scepticism?

"Hey, I think you're right. Certainly big enough. Well spotted. Took me years to see one of those."

The bird spiralled downwards and below the ridge.

"Not a bad way to finish your day, that. See the path down there? Half an hour and we should be down. Manage that OK?"

"No bother – but I'll try to go slow, considering your age."

"Thanks for that. I'll just take these boulders out of my rucksack then. So, enjoy that then? Bit of a challenge?"

"What challenge? Nothing to it. What'll we do tomorrow?"

Steve grinned. Looked like the kindling would catch.

Rob took another look round the pin-sharp perfection of the mountain landscape, watched the immaculate image of the magnificent bird diminish. Ahead he could see the flawless reproduction of the summit, a summit still clear in his memory. He clicked back on-screen, checked the time still left to go. His hand hovered over two of the buttons. Then pressed 'Cancel'.

LAND OF THE MOUNTAIN AND THE FLOOD

Beinn Achaladair – the mountain of the soaking field.
Mullach Cadha Rainich – the top of the dripping pass.
Beinn na Lap – the boggy mountain.
Meall nam Peitherin – the hill of the thunderbolts.

Rain from Heaven, rain from Hell,
Rain on mountain, rain on fell,
Cuts through soil, cuts through stone,
Cuts through flesh into the bone.

Sodden lochan, clag-soaked crag,
Slurping bog and black peat hag.
Soak and seep and drench and drain,
Water shed then shed again.

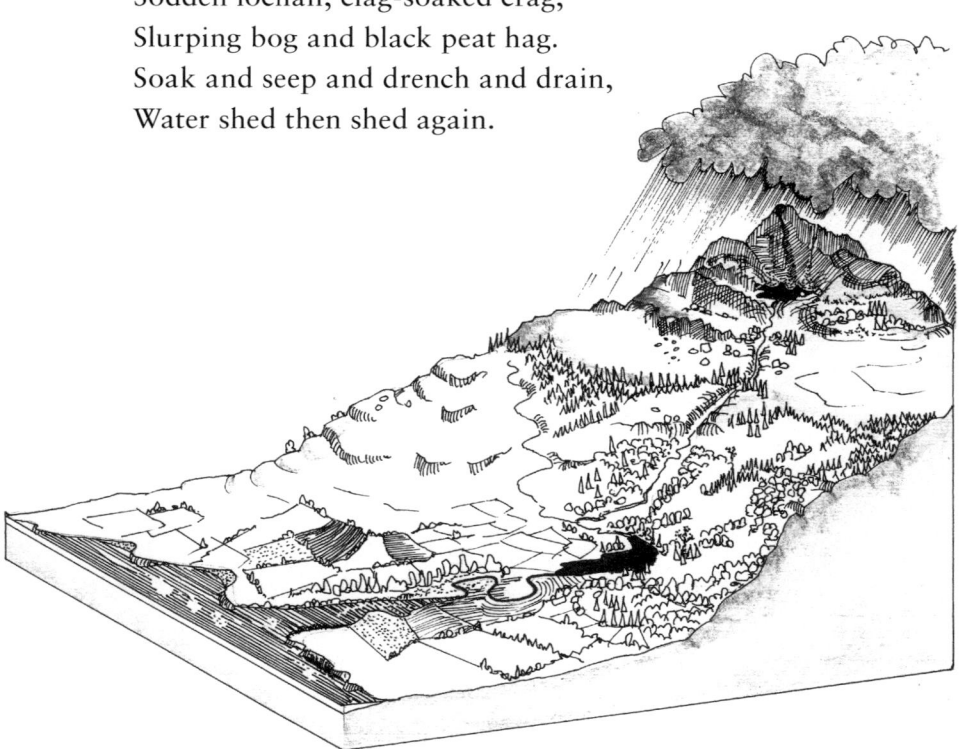

Mountains formed to gulp and swallow,
Spew into each dip and hollow.
Gullies flood, the burns pour,
Thunder echoes torrent roar.

Watercolour
Watermark,
Water light
Water dark,
Waterlogged
Watertight,
Water day
Water night.

Rain that softens, moistens, feeds,
Finds its way to deepest seeds.
Water falls, water rises,
Day and night the land baptises.

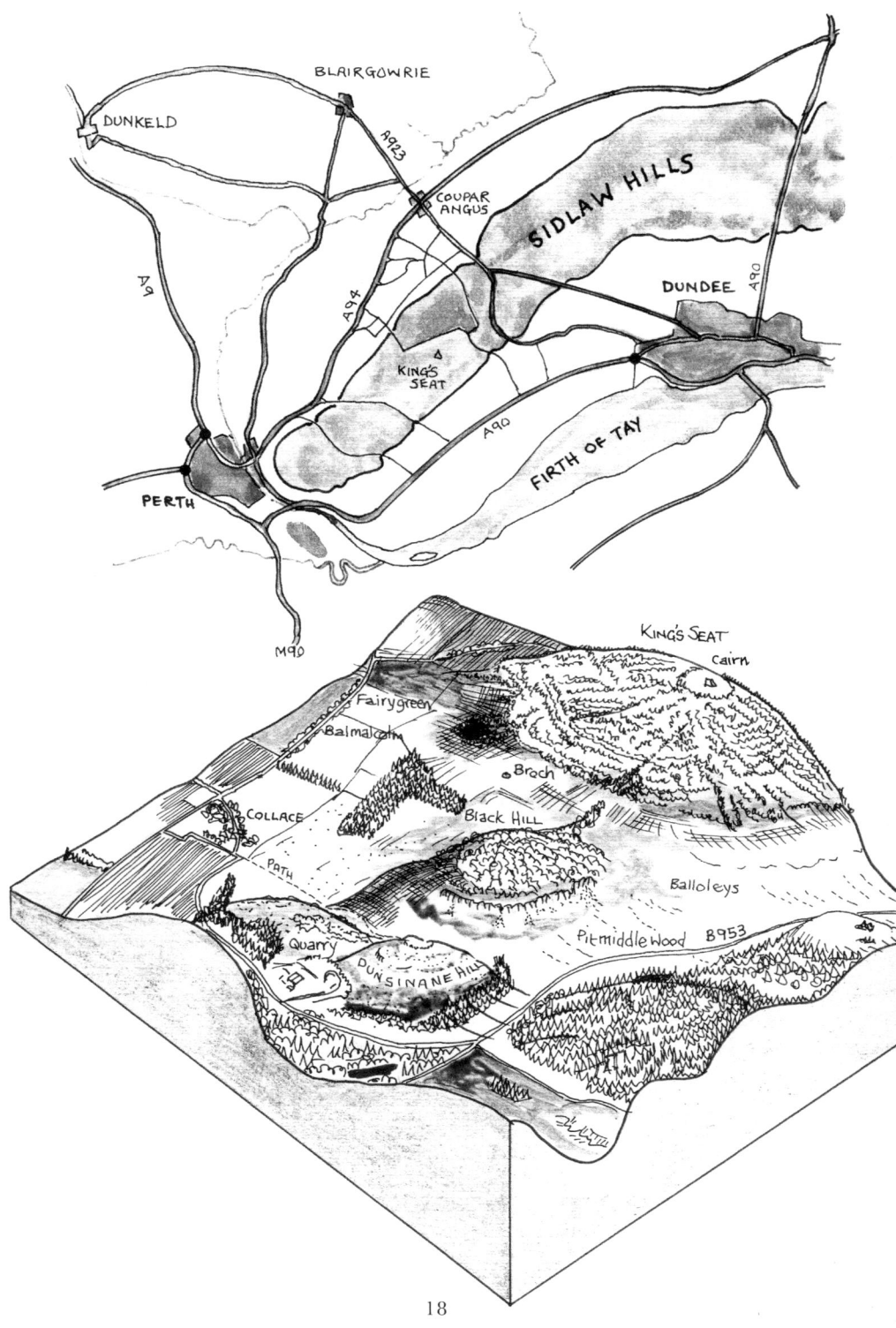

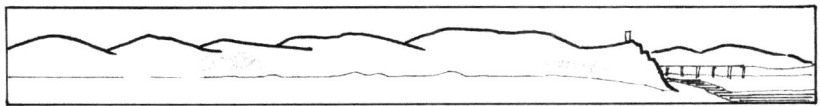

MACBETHADMACWHO?

As usual she glanced at the information board beside the gate, but didn't stop; she'd read it many times before. 'Macbeth's Castle?' was the heading, the question mark adding a note of honest doubt not always found on information boards. Once through the gate the path rose steeply, the challenging bit of the climb coming early.

For Katherine, Dunsinane – 'the hill of ants' – was *her* hill, starting no more than a couple of hundred metres from her home in Collace. She must have been up to the top scores of times over the years: first carried by her Dad; then holding her Mum's hand; nowadays on her own, something her friends at school found a 'totally weird' thing to do. Usually she carried a bit of chocolate, or maybe a drink. Today she carried the text of a play – *that* play – and a notepad. In fourth year now, her class had just finished reading *Macbeth*, an experience enjoyed by some, disliked by those who could not get past the 'stupid language', not to mention the idea of people speaking out loud with nobody listening – though that often happened with some teachers. Now she had an essay to write on the text and, not that she had told anyone, was climbing Dunsinane in the hope that it might somehow inspire her. 'Inspire' – she could just imagine using that word with her friends. Instant embarrassment.

The first bit of the hill took about four minutes, if you didn't stop. A bit like starting an essay, she thought, as she began the climb. Often the hardest part, but best not to hesitate. Now, as it levelled out a little, she could stop, catch her breath for a minute, and take in the patchwork of Perthshire laid out behind her. Straight behind was the hamlet of Collace. Over towards Blairgowrie a shimmer of light looked like a loch, but she now knew it to be an illusion – just the reflection of a large area of poly tents for the berries being grown there. The rest of the climb was now easier.

"Just like writing the main part of the essay," she said to herself. "A couple of false summits and a few sheep paths heading into irrelevance, but no problem if you knew where you were heading to. Hey, an extended image. Miss Mackintosh would like that."

As the summit neared she passed over what she now knew to be the grassy marker of the original Iron Age fort, then the outer rampart of the later fort, followed by its inner rampart, and finally the grassed over foundation of the defensive wall. Ripples, Katherine always imagined. Someone had dropped a stone on the saucer-like top of the hill and the overflowing ripples had been frozen, not in icy-blue but in green. Then time had covered and blurred what had once stood proud.

Walking round the circumference of the grassy mound Katherine could now see the full 360-degree panorama of Perthshire laid out around her. Sharp and clear till middle distance; hazy at the outer edges. She knew all the hills stretching in a line to the northeast – Black Hill, Little Dunsinane, King's Seat – but wasn't sure about those in the far distance. Turning from the view she sat down on the soft grass and brought out her book, hoping that reading it on top of Dunsinane might do something for her. After all, she had always felt that apart from the spectacular view there was just 'something about the place' which made it easy to imagine the past.

She turned to the start of Act 5 Scene 3, to the defiant Macbeth:

'Bring me no more reports; let them fly all.
Till Birnam wood remove to Dunsinane.
I cannot taint with fear...'

She turned and looked out in what she knew was the direction of Dunkeld and Birnam.

"Would have been a long way to carry a big branch in front of you," she thought. "Have to use that 'suspension of disbelief' Miss Mackintosh was always on about. And what about the way you had to pronounce Dunsinane? That iambic pentameter thingy made you say 'Dunsinane' to rhyme with 'rain', while locals always said 'Dun*sinnin*', like 'linen'. But then Shakespeare hadn't been up here to find that out, just looked at some maps. Anyway, she herself wasn't too hot on how to pronounce some of the Munros she had started to do with her Mum. It annoyed her a bit that she could remember English-sounding names like Ben Nevis or Ben Alder but could be climbing up some mountain with a Gaelic name and not be able to remember what it was.

She'd mentioned that to her mother one day, who had surprised her by replying:

'What's in a name? that which we call a rose
By any other name would smell as sweet.'

After her initial, "What are you on about?" Katherine had asked where these lines came from. "Is it a quote?" she had demanded, since quotations were gold in the mine of literature essays, bright nuggets to lay in tribute before the examiner.

"Of course it is. Haven't you read *Romeo and Juliet*?"

"Naw – some classes do that in fifth year. So...what are you saying? Doesn't matter what something's called. It's the...*thing* that matters?"

"The Bard couldn't have put it better himself, sweetie. The mountain, the rose – they don't change."

As she remembered this pearl she became aware of another visitor arriving at the hill-top. She had neither seen nor heard him approaching, he just appeared at the edge of her vision. A man, an old man, a man categorised by her generation as a 'crumblie'. Katherine herself had occasionally used that term when with her friends, but rather enjoyed the company of older people. This one conformed to various stereotypes – beard, beige jacket, bunnet – but this impression was offset by a gaze which suggested more life than she saw in the eyes of some of her peers.

He sat down a few yards away, legs bent, arms resting on knees.

"Good morning m'dear."

"Hi. Nice day, eh?"

"Indeed it is. A good day for many things – for enjoying a fine view and reading a good book. Is it a good book?"

"Well it's Shakespeare, so I suppose that makes it good. *Macbeth*. Bit cheesy reading it up here I suppose. You know, Dunsinane and that?"

"So will you be writing about this play for an exam then?"

"Maybe. But now we're doing an essay on the reasons he became so evil. You know, killing everybody just because of ambition. And getting other people to kill even women and children. Or was it his wife that pushed him? Or the witches? All that stuff."

"Ah, so it's Shakespeare's character Macbeth you are to write about? Not Mac Bethad mac Findlaich?"

"Macbethadmacwho?"

"Mac Bethad mac Findlaich, the Mormaer of Moray. Ruler of Alba for seventeen prosperous years. Have your teachers not told you about him? You would like him I'm sure. A much nicer man than your 'tyrant' and 'butcher'. And his wife Queen Gruoch, a fine woman. Not at all a 'fiend-like queen' I'm glad to say."

"What, is that who they were in, like, history? You mean the story's not true? Shakespeare just made up stuff?"

"Well you could say it's *his* story but not history. But you can't just blame the English Bard. I'm afraid it all really started within Scotland. You'll have heard that 'the winners write history'. Well, some time after his death it became useful for Scottish historians to re-fashion Mac Bethad's history to suit the latest winners. Och, I'm afraid I'm going to bore you."

Nigel wondered if this role-play was such a good idea.

"No, no, it's interesting. Go on. Please."

"Well these historians, their propaganda became taken as fact, and by the time Shakespeare dipped into his sources for a Scottish story Mac Bethad was now a tyrant. And the rest… has become a *kind* of history."

"But that's not fair. I just thought it was all real. What else is wrong?"

The old man smiled and rose. "Tell me your name first. Then you can help me down the hill. I'm fine getting up if I take my time but I have to watch my step going down. What's that, Katherine is it? You can call me Mac. Very appropriate isn't it? And we'll call Mac Bethad Macbeth, since that's what you're used to."

Their descent, as Katherine asked more questions about the

play, was like walking down scree. Each step pushed aside hard facts, crunched received wisdom underfoot. The solid nuggets of memorised characterisation notes were buried beneath mini-avalanches of new information.

"Did Macbeth kill Duncan when he was asleep?"

"No, Katherine, Duncan died in battle, at a place now called Pitgaveny, invading Macbeth's territory. Macbeth *might* have been the one to kill him, but we don't know that."

"What about Duncan? Had he been a good king?"

"Not a very successful one. Scotland was much more peaceful and prosperous under Macbeth. And for seventeen long years, which was a long time to reign in those days."

"Did Macbeth have anything to do with... witches and stuff?"

"Unlikely, m'dear. He was the first Scottish king to make a pilgrimage to Rome. I don't think the Pope would have approved of him taking advice from witches."

"But what about Lady Macbeth? What was she really like?"

"Gruoch? By all accounts a clever, pragmatic woman who gave generously to the Church. Protective of her son, Lulach. He was Macbeth's stepson and Macbeth even allowed Lulach to take over from him as king, though the young man was killed a year later. So Macbeth had to take over again. Then he himself was killed in battle with the Malcolm who is in your play, a few months later. But not here. At a place called Lumphanan, in what we now call Aberdeenshire. There is a story told that after defeating his enemy Malcolm placed Macbeth's sword on the ground, placed his own on top, at right-angles, and danced a victory jig around them. And so we have the famous Sword Dance."

"Was that true?"

"Well, it is no taller a tale than many told about Macbeth."

"This is just confusing," said Katherine. "What *was* true?

What about this hill? Was Macbeth never here?"

"Oh yes, he did come here when retreating from English invaders under Siward – yes, there was a Siward, just as Shakespeare wrote. But Dunsinane was just a hill-fort, not a place where he stayed."

Katherine looked around her. The only things she thought she could now trust were what she could see around her: the stones and grass beneath her feet; the green ridges of the fort still visible above her; anything close enough to touch and feel and know for reality. And the old man. She felt she could trust him.

"How do you know all this stuff?" she asked. "Were you a history teacher?"

"No, no, nothing so clever as that. I just happen to have picked up a bit of knowledge about this – over the years."

They reached the bottom of the hill, the little lay-by at the corner of the road where cars parked, but which was currently empty.

"Did you not drive here?"

"No, no. Never liked cars. Walking's fine for me. It's been good talking to you Katherine. Maybe I'll see you again. I'm around here often. And remember – don't believe everything you see or everything you read."

And with that he walked to the bend of the road and disappeared around it, as quietly as he had earlier appeared.

That evening, over tea, she mentioned her meeting with the old man and what he had told her.

"It was funny", she said. "He was like someone from a different century, like one of those wise old men you get in books, that always know stuff nobody else does. And the way he appeared then just disappeared round the corner."

"Sounds very mysterious," said her Mum.

"What was he wearing?" asked her Dad. "Brown jacket, shirt without a collar, bunnet with a pheasant feather?"

"How did you know that?"

"That was Jack McLean. He's a local amateur historian. Knows everything about Dunsinane. And seems to know everything about Scottish history. He lives just up the road from the Collace Quarry."

"Oh, right," said Katherine.

Of course she'd known there was nothing really mysterious about the man she'd met, who seemed to have come from nowhere and then just disappeared. Of course she'd known. But somehow, just somehow, she preferred what her imagination had half created.

Later, she settled down to start her essay. 'Discuss the most important reasons for Macbeth's descent into evil.' Unusually for her she just could not get started. The two Macbeths were in her mind, locked in combat. Eventually she typed out, 'Although the Macbeth in Shakespeare's play certainly became evil there is another Macbeth who was a good king.'

Then she stopped, sighed, and deleted. Starting again she

typed, 'By the end of the play Macbeth was well described as 'this dead butcher'. He killed and gave orders to kill. There are many reasons...'

Again she stopped, her fingers hovering over the keyboard. What had Miss Mackintosh said? 'Don't just regurgitate your notes. Try to let the person reading know what *you* think.'

She hit delete and typed once more. 'Mac Bethad mac Findlaich ruled for seventeen prosperous years. Unlike Shakespeare's character Macbeth, who will be dealt with later, he was anything but evil, and his wife...'

Near Shinigag

A greylag goose on a sliver of water,
Pushing its reflection into the shallows.
Above, a partner checks air, water, land.
Two geese: bird of water and bird of air
In a glen of crag and burn and lochan.
Transition from air to water begins,
A mobile crisis of identity.
Silent descent, slapstick water-walking,
Sudden shattering of surface tension,
Emerging to quiet and calm control.
Now an arrogant glide that turns its back
On the ruffled white feathers behind,
Nodding to the swaying, dipping reeds.
Two greylag geese on a sliver of water,
Feeding together, in silence, backs turned.

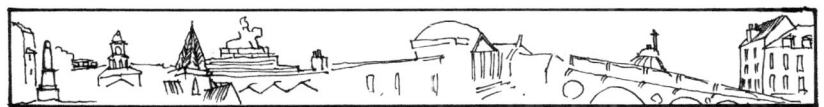

FAIR CITY FRIENDS

"Good morning Walter. How are you today?" she asked. "And Maida. Faithful as ever, looking up at your master." Citizens of the Fair City walking along Marshall Place paid no heed to the bird-like figure of Jean Scott, local historian and distant relative of the famed novelist and poet, looking up at his statue and engaging him in friendly conversation.

"Good morning to you, Jean. You're looking well. Off for a walk are you?"

"I am. It's time to look up some of my friends. I haven't seen some of them for quite a while. But before I go, Walter, I've always wanted to know, do you enjoy standing here or did you prefer your old situation at the bottom of the High Street?"

Walter considered the question. Behind him stretched the green expanse of the South Inch; to his right, across King's Place, stood the compact bulk of St Leonard's-in-the-Fields Church, its crown-spire modelled on that of Edinburgh's High Kirk of St Giles, in front of which stood yet another statue of himself. To his left he could see the railway bridge behind which lay Perth Station. If the city fathers of 1845 had not encountered such fierce opposition from the townspeople then that station would have been right behind him, on the Inch. Barbarism. His view to the right took in the Georgian symmetry of the Marshall Place terraces, reminding him of his days in Edinburgh. Had he preferred the hustle and bustle of the High Street?

"A difficult question, Jean. I liked seeing all the people on the High Street and making up tales around them, just for my own amusement you know. But here I have the bonny crocuses in Spring, I can hear the children playing on the Inch – and Maida likes to speak to the dogs that get walked here. No, this is a fine place for a man of my age. And people are very civilised here. I'm told that bronze of 'The Fair Maid of Perth', you know the one in the High Street, has a terrible time. Hats and gloves on her, containers of ale put in her hands. Strangers wrapping their arms round her. Quite undignified. No wonder she looks so nervous."

"She does, doesn't she? Always looks like a poor wee wallflower not expecting to get asked for a dance. But I'm glad you're happy here, Walter. Now excuse me if you may, I must get along. Goodbye, my friend."

Statue of Walter Scott.

Miss Scott walked towards the river, shutting out the noise of the traffic and remembering how much quieter things had been here eighty years ago when she was a child, playing on the Inch with her sisters. As she reached the River Tay end of Marshall Place she noticed a familiar figure across the road from the Fergusson Gallery, gazing up at the domed rotunda. The one-time waterworks had been built in the style of a Graeco-Roman temple, not something likely to happen today, thought Miss Scott. After a spell as the Tourist Office it was now a gallery housing the works of J.D. Fergusson, the celebrated Scottish Colourist painter.

"Professor Anderson, how nice to see you. Looking on your works but not despairing, I hope."

"Miss Scott, good morning. Just having a look at what they've done to the place. I'm not sure this female figure they've put in front would have been allowed in my day. Not quite respectable for it to be shown *outside* the gallery. But they have made a fine job of the conversion."

Professor Adam Anderson, thought Jean, must have been one

of the busiest men in Scotland. He had been Rector of Perth Academy for twenty-eight years, introducing science into the curriculum, then Professor of Natural Philosophy at the University of St Andrews. In his idle hours he had been instrumental in bringing gas lighting to Perth, involved in the improvement of the port at Friarton, and had designed not only the system to pump water from the Tay but the building he was now looking at, whose dome housed the cistern storing the water.

'*Aquam Igne Aqua Haurio*' read the Latin motto above the door – I draw water by fire and water. The power of steam; quite a romantic thought nowadays. Miss Scott could remember well the distinctive chuff-chuff sound of the steam trains entering and leaving Perth.

"Are you sorry to see your building as a gallery now?"

"Not at all, Miss Scott. *Tempus fugit*, as some of my pupils might have been able to translate. Time flies. Nearly two hundred years now and still being looked after, unlike some of the buildings in Perth. I believe St Paul's is in a terrible state. No, I'm very happy, very happy indeed."

Bidding the professor farewell Miss Scott rounded the corner into Tay Street and crossed the road. Tay Street, with its strikingly attractive floodwall and fine array of public art, was one of her favourite places to walk. And of all the pieces of street decoration her favourite was the little line of green and black and orange creatures to be found on the section of the wall between the Railway Bridge and Canal Street. No doubt they puzzled many tourists, unaware that they represented quirky creatures from one of William Soutar's bairnrhymes. As a young woman Miss Scott had visited the bedridden Perth poet at his home in Wilson Street, before his untimely death in 1943.

"Hello Willie," she now said to herself. "I'm sorry you can't see how many of your words you'd find around Perth now, cut into stone and metal would you believe." She thought of the Tay Street pillars – the child-friendly verses from *Aince Upon a Day* and the life-affirming extract from *Autobiography*, which read:

'Into a bed, into a room:
Out of a garden, into a town,
And to a country, and up and down
The earth;'

She thought too of David Annand's *Soutar Ring*, the two figures in the ring in the High Street. And on that ring the words of *Nae Day Sae Dark*:

'Nae day sae dark; nae wud sae bare;
Nae grund sae stour wi' stane;
But licht comes through; a sang is there;
A glint o' grass is green.'

"All that suffering you tholed, and still that optimism," she thought. "I wish I'd been allowed to know you longer."

She walked on past the Sheriff Court, thinking of its architect, Robert Smirke, who had also been responsible for the British Museum and Covent Garden Theatre. Justice, History and the Arts – a good heritage to leave. To her right was the Queen's Bridge, an exercise in plain functionality if ever there was one. She preferred to look upriver to the arched splendour of Smeaton's Bridge. "Why can't we have both functionality and attractiveness?" she thought.

Then she was reminded of the City Hall, stuck in planning permission limbo, delay being the most definite decision so far made regarding its future.

"Some think it's functional but not attractive," she mused. "Then others think it's attractive but not functional. And some think it's both, or neither. No wonder it's a problem."

As she moved on, admiring the river, she heard behind her a

most peculiar sound. Poetry? Well words which rhymed anyway. Too polite to turn round and stare she listened to the declamation:

'Beautiful Ancient City of Perth,
One of the fairest on the earth,
With your stately mansions and scenery most fine,
Which seems very beautiful in the summer time;
And the beautiful silvery Tay,
Rolling smoothly on its way,
And glittering like silver in the sunshine -
And the Railway Bridge across it is really sublime.'

"My goodness," she whispered to herself. "It's McGonagall. William Topaz McGonagall. Thank heavens I didn't turn round. I might have been given a further recitation. I'd forgotten that he moved from Dundee to Perth for a short while. I suppose we should be glad that he liked our *'Beautiful Ancient City'*, but perhaps if he'd liked it less there would have been less 'poetry'. Strange, strange man."

Miss Scott made sure not to turn her head and make eye contact with 'The Poet Laureate of the Silvery Tay' (that's the *Dundee Courier* for you). After all, she'd read *The Ancient Mariner* and knew what might happen. But at the High Street junction a more welcome figure was found, standing beside the new Council Chambers, formerly the headquarters of the General Accident Fire & Life Assurance Corporation. Sir Francis Norie-Miller, dynamic chairman of General Accident, Justice of the Peace, Chairman of the School Board of Perth and of Perth Infirmary. Liberal MP for a brief period – like Adam Anderson he was a man who clearly did not like having time on his hands. As a young girl Miss Scott had loved to see the colourful array of flags flying from the window-ledges of the General Accident building, one for every one of the over-fifty countries with which the company did business.

On seeing Miss Scott a smile appeared beneath the military-style moustache. "Jean, how pleasant to see you. Out for a stroll?"

"Just a short one, Sir Francis. I like to get out every day if I can, but I don't have the same energy I used to have. But I was walking through the Norie-Miller Walk. It's looking bonnier than ever. A lovely way to remember your son."

"Indeed, proud of young Stanley, very proud. Carried on the business and also something left for the people of Perth to enjoy."

"They've made a grand job of improving the whole of Riverside Park. And I'm even getting used to some of that terribly modern stuff on the Sculpture Trail."

"Good for you, always keep an open mind. People thought I was mad when I targeted car insurance, but look at that business now. Move with the times, Miss Scott, move with the times, move with the times, move with the times…"

"Is she… Is she, away?"

"Not yet, but may not be long, I'm afraid. But she's a fighter, you can tell. Her lips keep moving, she seems to be talking to herself. Then it stops. But there she goes again."

"What do you think she's saying?"

"No idea, I'm afraid. But she smiles every now and then. She's not in pain."

"Where is this now? I was talking to Sir Francis, wasn't I, and now I'm, where?..." She was standing at the top of George Street looking across at the Museum & Art Gallery. She couldn't remember getting here, but that was happening more often these days.

"Are you all right, Jean? Perhaps come in for some water?"

She looked up at the figure she knew so well, resplendent in his breeches and carelessly-draped cloak. Thomas Hay Marshall who, along with his father-in-law Thomas Anderson, had been mainly responsible for the development of Georgian Perth. Now he stood in the portico of the Museum, above which could be read the inscription, *'T. H. Marshall, Cives Grati'*. The citizens had indeed been grateful, raising the money for the statue by public subscription.

"Och, I'm fine now, Thomas. Just took a little turn there, but quite myself again. It's a fine spot you have there, but I hope you don't get kept awake by the performances in the Concert Hall. They can be very noisy."

"Not at all, I like to hear what's going on – and I like a lot of this new music. That Tina Turner show was a rare thing."

Miss Scott was glad to hear him in such good humour, given the 'problem' with his young wife Rose. At the Atholl Street end of Rose Terrace, for the Terrace had been named after her, was a townhouse intended for the couple but lived in by neither of them. Lord Elgin, of the Elgin Marbles fame, had lodgings opposite the Marshalls and when Thomas was away on business Rose and Elgin engaged in a less than clandestine affair. Rose proved to be 'no better than she should be', later dallying with a military doctor then, having moved to Edinburgh, with various officers of the Royal Artillery. Like her husband Rose had been a very busy person.

"Poor Thomas," thought Miss Scott. "But thankfully two hundred years is enough to get over it."

She began to walk up the final stretch of George Street, looking forward to turning towards that view of the North Inch stretching out towards the hills in the distance, flanked on one side by the busy waters of the Tay, on the other by the calm dignity of Rose Terrace. She turned to walk but found it difficult to get her legs moving.

"Seems to be having a rest; she's less agitated now. Hopefully she'll sleep for a while."

Miss Scott woke up to find herself sitting on one of the benches between the statue of Prince Albert and the Lynedoch Monument, on the corner of the North Inch.

"Goodness, I seem to be getting from place to place, but I wish I could remember the journey. Never mind, it's not a bad place to wake up. A place of memories."

And indeed it was such a place. Perth's Memorial Garden. Military memories mostly: reminders of courage, of sacrifice, of regimental history. The most poignant perhaps was the memorial to the 51st Highland Division. Alan Herriot's bronze statue showed a young Dutch girl presenting a rose to a kilted Highland soldier. He carried bagpipes, not a rifle. Across the North Sea in Schijndel, Holland, was an identical bronze commemorating that town's liberation by the Highlanders. Not far away, on either side of the floodgates, were two more memorials: one for the employees of the Perth Co-operative Society who died in the two world wars; one for the men and women of Perthshire who fought in the International Brigades in Spain against fascism.

Miss Scott walked slowly across to talk to another of her friends, the man associated with the Lynedoch Monument.

"Thomas Graham – you'll forgive me if I don't call you Baron Lynedoch. We have something in common after all, do we not? Your dear, beautiful wife died when only thirty-five; my David was taken from me by the war, and only twenty-five. We both had to fill the rest of our lives without them. You lived on till ninety-six; I have managed ninety-four, though I fear I will not overtake you. But you, Thomas, filled your life with military adventures. You were the hero of Barossa, Wellington's second-in-command. You made history. I have been content to read it. But it's been my life, and I've met so many people through it."

"And look what you have achieved, Jean. All those hundreds of Perth pupils growing up knowing more about their city, realising how much has happened here, how many of its citizens have achieved great things in the world. You should be proud. They should name a street after you."

"Ah well, Walter got their first. Of course I could always claim Jeanfield Road, but I believe that name comes from 'Gin Field' and I'm not sure if my mother would have approved of that."

"Nonsense, nothing the matter with a bit of gin; that would suit me fine. Better perhaps to be associated with a gin-field than a battle-field such as Barossa. There have been too many battles, too much fighting."

Behind her she heard the clan war-cries of the Chattans and the Kays as they rushed towards each other across the Inch to settle a feud in bloody conflict; the battering down of the door to the chamber of James I by his assassins; the screaming of the mobs as they sacked Perth's religious houses, inflamed by Knox's sermon against idolatry in St John's Kirk; the crash of falling masonry as Cromwell tore down the Mercat Cross to supply stone for his Citadel on the South Inch; the metallic clang of claymore and targe as the Jacobite armies of '15 and '45 assembled on the North Inch.

"Can you not calm her doctor? Look at her – she's shaking now."

"I'm going to increase the sedative. But she's slipping away. It'll be peaceful."

She was sitting in St John's Kirk now, in her usual place. Looking round she could see so many people she knew: David Douglas back from a plant-hunting expedition, Salvador Ysart holding one of his pieces of glass, Patrick Geddes, Arthur Bell, Joan Knight, David Ogston…And the music – not hymns but Jacobite songs from Lady Nairne of Gask, the swooping fiddle of Niel Gow, the defiant singing of the suffragettes outside Perth prison, the young voices of the Jambouree Choir and the Fair City Singers. Now the bells, the carillon of St John, such a sound, such a joyful sound.

*'St Johnstoun's bells ring bonnie
And awaken echoes many.'*

Such a sound…

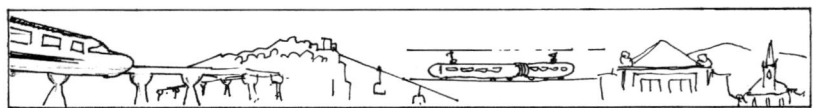

PERTH 2040

THE SILVER BULLET-TRAIN decelerated smoothly and glided into Perth station. Jenny Scott looked at the display on the headrest in front of her. *14:14, 21.05.40.* Twenty-five minutes from Edinburgh. Impressive. She vaguely remembered train journeys from Perth to the capital as a child. An hour and a half? Two hours? A long time anyway, and for some reason travelling via Stirling. Her family had emigrated to Canada when she was just fifteen. Although she was aware of many of the changes in Scotland over the intervening twenty years, the only Perth which made the news was the Canadian Perth, in Ontario. So not only was she looking forward to seeing her uncle Walter, she also wondered how Perth might have changed.

Walter, instantly recognisable from his *Personphile* images, greeted her at the passenger reception area with an all-enveloping hug and a stream of questions. Once they had been dealt with they took the *Citytram* the short distance to his flat overlooking the South Inch Leisure Park.

"Now lass, what d'you fancy doing this afternoon? Have a rest or a go for a walk? And would you stop calling me Uncle Walter. Makes me feel even older."

"OK Walter. I'd love a walk around the city, see what I remember."

"Come on then, let's give you the tour. That's a bonny Canadian accent you've got, by the way. But there's maybe a bit of Scottish still in there."

As they made their way up the Edinburgh Road she looked over at the Lesser South Inch, no longer open parkland as she remembered but now dotted with air-skate ramps, outdoor exercise equipment, and other recreational facilities.

"We used to go to the Highland Games there. Does that still happen?"

"Indeed it does, but it's too big an event for the Inch. Ever since the Heavyweight events were included as an Olympic sport there's been a huge increase in attendance, so the Games are held in McDiarmid Park. People come from all over."

"Oh, that's the football stadium isn't it? Dad still talks about going to see the Saints. How are they doing?"

"The Saints? Near the top of the Premier League again, and still in Europe. Lots of big-money transfers nowadays, ever since they got the sponsorship from the BBC."

"The BBC? I thought I read that they'd been privatised and were called something different now."

"Correct. But I'm talking about the Bertha Bioinformatics Corporation. You'll have heard of them, no doubt. Multinational now. They've put a lot of money and good jobs into Perth, including our sports teams. You don't see many buses leaving Perth to go and watch other teams nowadays. They had to add capacity to McDiarmid a few years ago. Football still not big in Canada then?"

"Soccer? It's pretty big, but we still like our hockey."

"So it's 'we' now, Jenny? Feel Canadian, do you?"

"It's kind of funny. I feel Canadian back in Vancouver but coming back here is…I don't know, a bit like coming home. I guess I've forgotten a lot but still remember things too…But I don't remember that, Walter. That's new."

They had reached the corner of Tay Street by now and Jenny was pointing up towards the long, wooded top of Kinnoull Hill. Her attention was taken by the series of metallic supports carrying a cable which glinted in the mid-afternoon sunshine. Suspended from this cable a rectangular cabin travelled just above the treeline.

"That, m'dear, is the *Kinnoull Kable Car*. Kinnoull and Kable with a 'K'. They were going to spell Car with a 'K' as well then decided 'KKK' might be a bad idea. Still a few people who know their history. I hate the spelling but I must admit that it's been great for the tourism. You get taken along the top of the hill then steep down over the Dundee road. When you get to the bottom, at Friarton Quay – they wanted to call it Friarton Key, with another 'K' but thank God that wasn't allowed – when you get there you can transfer to one of the *Kinnoull Kruisers* and take a trip up to Dundee."

"That'll be *Kruisers* with a 'K' I guess."

"Got it in one. Bit of an obsession with that letter. I believe it's meant to look 'forward - thinking, thrustful and dynamic'. Stupid, more like. Mr McLaren, my old English teacher at the Academy, wouldn't have approved. But again it's been great for tourists, and Perth folk too. They like a wee day trip up the Tay to McGonagall Quay in Dundee, even though the shopping's meant to be better in Perth now."

Huh! There's nothing to do around here!

"McGonagall. Was he that funny poet? Mum used to go on about him and 'the beautiful silvery Tay'."

"Ah, yes, not very funny if you like poetry but that was your man. And that was one of his classics:

*'Beautiful silvery Tay,
With your landscapes, so lovely and gay.
Along each side of your waters, to Perth all the way.'*

Very fond of the adjective 'Beautiful', especially in his titles. *Beautiful Aberfoyle, Beautiful Balmerino, Beautiful Balmoral* and, I believe, another dozen or so. Even *Beautiful Torquay*. But he's mostly forgotten now. If you *infoquest* him now the first reference you get is that Minerva McGonagall character from those Harry Potter books you used to read."

They walked on towards the Queen's Bridge, now eighty years old but which, till the Fair City Bridge near Scone was opened, had always been referred to as 'the new bridge'. Jenny was struck by the lack of traffic. Trams slid quietly past at regular intervals but the only other vehicles were small electric cars and bigger vans, both carrying the distinctive double-headed eagle of the Perth coat of arms, and shoals of bicycles travelling in Perspex-roofed lanes.

"No private cars allowed nowadays, Walter?"

"Not since the integrated transport system came in – when was it? – in 2030. There's a big circle of park and rides round the city – some of them are underground. Then there are the hubs in all of the city districts. The *Subhubs*. You get *Citytrams* for free and the *Citycars* are heavily subsidised. All the goods vehicles go to the transport hubs on the, what d'ye call them… arterial roads, then their loads are distributed by *Cityvans*. It was controversial at the time and certainly cost a lot to set up, but the economic returns have been substantial. Plus the environmental benefits."

"Yeah, that's pretty similar to our set-up in Vancouver, though we bring in a lot of stuff by boat too."

"Yes, we're a bit ahead of the game here in Perth. Though I believe Edinburgh'll soon be finished their tram extension down to Leith. We've gone as green as possible over the years. You'll see our logo everywhere: *Perth – the Green Heart of Scotland*. Right, let's take you into the centre and we can get you a coffee."

They turned left into South Street, past the Tommy Wright statue, and then right, into King Edward Street, stopping outside the front entrance of the City Hall.

"You'll remember this building?" asked Walter, smiling.

"Kind of, but I was never inside. It had been shut up for years. Were they not trying to knock it down? And was it not all grey and a bit boring?"

"Some people thought so. Other folk liked it. But you don't think it looks boring now?"

"No way, it looks fantastic. All that glass and greenery. And the water coming down from the roof."

"They got a young team from the V&A Museum of Design in Dundee to take on the project. Must have started just after you and your folks left. Come on inside for a coffee. And since it's Friday we should get a bit of music too."

The foyer was laid out with advertising material and samples for Perthshire shops and attractions. An information and volunteering station for local organisations took up one corner. Inside, the main area of tables and chairs were laid out round a central coffee bar.

"The coffee bar's on a platform," said Walter. "It can be wheeled out of the road if needed."

Up on a raised stage a young jazz quartet were finishing a mellow set, to be replaced by an even younger string group.

"Local talent," explained Walter. "Usually young folk from the schools or the music college, or just up-and-coming musicians who get a platform, literally, to be heard. There's a lot of music made in Perth – always has been – and we get to hear more of it now. All sorts of styles. Mind, though – they had to suggest to one bunch of girls that customers might find conversation difficult. *Retrometal* I think they called themselves."

After their coffee they moved into the outside corridors where hung the fifty or so art works representing Perth from earliest times up to the present day, all with short, informative captions.

"It was an idea they got from *The Great Tapestry of Scotland*. Ever hear of that?"

"Yeah, I remember that. I think it had just been finished a couple of years before we left."

"Well Perth has got a huge amount of history, so a list of events and people was drawn up and then older school pupils and college students were given the job of creating the images in whatever medium they wanted. It's a great draw now for locals and visitors, and it lets kids here know what a lot has happened here. Sometimes the artists had to use their imaginations of course, for the things way back in time."

They wandered past paintings of what Perth Castle might have looked like before it was swept away by flood, of Robert the Bruce wading across the Lade by night to recapture the city, of the bloody Battle of the Clans on the North Inch. Next came *The Fair Maid of Perth*, for some reason in Andy Warhol style. There were video installations too – of the winning goal in Saints' first Scottish Cup win of 2014 and of the great Bridgend fire of 2028. Then came a bust of Patrick Geddes, a collage of Perth's twelve twin towns, a portrait of Scotland's First Minister – a proud son of Perth. Round the walls rolled Perth's history.

"These are great, Uncle...I mean Walter. You forget all this stuff happened here."

"I'm sure, but if you want to see a bit of what's going on nowadays why don't we walk along to *The Perthshire Experience*.

It's in part of the Theatre complex. They've converted an area into a kind of 3D cinema thing and they show films about Perthshire. Busy place in the summer, especially when it's raining, but we should be all right today."

Walking along the High Street they passed the Ibbeson bronze of *The Fair Maid of Perth*.

"I do remember her," said Jenny. "She always looked a bit sad, and I see she's still got her permatan."

At the Mill Street entrance Walter bought tickets for the next showing, which was in twenty minutes, giving them time to look around the *Theatrical Memorabilia Gallery*. When they eventually took their seats in the small auditorium Jenny, tired after her journey, thought that she might fall asleep – until the opening of the film dispelled all such notions. A drone camera swooped down the Tay from Dundee at high speed, the Carse of Gowrie flashing past. Climbing upwards the camera homed in on the sights of Perth and its locality: the Kinnoull Tower, watching over the river traffic; Moncrieffe Hill with its restored hill forts; Scone Palace, showing no sign of the underpass below its grounds, leading to The Fair City Bridge; the roof gardens of the expanded Museum & Art Gallery, home to the Stone of Destiny. Then stomachs were challenged by the three-dimensional impressions of 'becoming' a golf ball arcing down a fairway, an osprey diving towards the Loch of the Lowes, a bungee jumper plummeting downwards from the River Garry Bridge, a skier slaloming down the Dunsinane artificial slope. The next section brought to life many of the historical events associated with the area, becoming less bloodthirsty as the centuries rolled on. Assassinations, clan battles and riots gave way to civic improvements. Destruction and looting changed to town planning and flood defences. Finally the film made sure its viewers were made aware of the business, shopping and entertainment possibilities in Perth and the wider area.

As she and her uncle were leaving the theatre Jenny's head was filled with images – some familiar, some half-remembered, many new to her.

"I guess I'm not going to fit in everything that I want to see, Walter. A week's not going to be enough, is it?"

"Well you'll just have to come back again. You'll always be welcome. Anyway, let's get you back to the flat. That's enough for one day."

Standing at the tram stop Walter drew Jenny's attention to a small bust and plaque set into the wall behind her, one of several they had seen that day featuring sons and daughters of the Fair City.

"Just one more thing you might be interested in. Do you see the name, there?"

"Let me have a look. *Jean Scott 1922-2016. Local historian and great friend of Perth.*' Hey, is she the one I've heard about? My, what is it, great-great-aunt?"

"Indeed she is. And a link between you and my famous namesake, Walter. She did more than anyone to make sure Perth knew its history."

Jenny looked more closely, eyes dropping to the lines etched into the plaque:

'So sing of our history, of days gone by,
Then sing of our future, our spirits high.
Let us learn from our past so our future is bright.
There are chapters of history which we can write.'

"What's the poem, Walter?"

"I believe it was a song. Written for a young choir to sing back in 2010, when Perth celebrated the 800-year anniversary of receiving its second Royal Charter. Miss Scott always liked the lines from it and it seemed to sum up her attitude to history: learn from it, but don't get stuck in it. Apparently she could have some very radical opinions, despite her very respectable appearance."

"That's so cool. I've finally met my great-great-aunt. Kind of. I wonder what she'd make of her Perth now?"

The tram drew up and they entered. Walter checked his *wristpad* for a quick check of the local news and weather. 'New plans announced for St Paul's Church', ran one line.

"Aye," he thought, "some things never change."

In Your Place

Cows may look at you with curiosity,
Lacking the disadvantage of manners,
As you stride straight past, going nowhere fast.
They pause from their evening ruminations
And stare, with gentle eyes faintly puzzled,
At this figure who flaps so clumsily
At his attentive escort of midges.
Musing on your place in their scheme of things
Lasts only a few motionless seconds.
Your lack of significance registered
The heads swing down again, the tongues emerge,
The tails swish lazily and efficiently.

Morning Walk

In a cage of spars and chicken-wire,
Floor stinking with fly-blown offal,
A crow explodes from bar to bar,
Its beak red raw, feathers crumpled,
Sparing the shepherd from the sight
Of lambs with eyes pecked clean.

By the path two deer lie gralloched,
Broken barrels with white-bleached staves
Pointing up to the sodden sky
And away from the burn's grey stones,
Each culled to protect the survivors
Of the herd in the corrie above

Death and Life in the Mountain

THE GREY POWDER was scattered. Some settled on the bracken and the tussocks, waiting for rain to carry it downwards. Some clung camouflaged on quartzite rocks, as if drawn by their shared origin of metamorphosing heat. Puffs of breeze took some further, across and down the flanks of the mountain, now dispersed so finely that no camouflage was needed. Darkness fell. Rain fell. Ash melded into mountain.

First, just the cycles of the year were felt. The clean chill of winters was a stronger sensation than the stuttering, half-hearted warmth of most summers. Springs crept in uncertainly: stealthy intimations of life, then a quivering impulse towards light and air. And quiet, unsettling, was the closing down into death or hibernation of autumns.

Time passed. A plaque rusted, was cleaned, rusted again. And more subtle messages made themselves known – felt most clearly where the ash had fallen thickest; shadowy where it had separated most finely. The infinitesimal settling of gravel and pebble; the reluctant drip from thawing icicle tip; even the ghost touch of smirr.

Incrementally, like a foetus forming, a kind of identity returned. It grew stronger, until he finally comprehended an awareness of himself, a new self which had merged and fused with the mountain, yet was separate from it. Like a blind man learning Braille he became familiar with the calligraphy of his surroundings – every cleft and crevice, every fissure, and fault and fracture. Now he could recognise life: the scouring of the burns in spate; the rooted tapestry of heather, bracken, pine, rowan. He felt death too: rotted trunks and branches; chick-skeleton leavings of carrion crow; deer put to sleep by winter. And another kind of death – he felt it pluck at what was a kind of memory, but a memory his identity sensed yet could not name.

Time grew further. He was aware of something which some part of him remembered as a voice, a voice whispering. Whispering just a sound, then in something he knew as words. The words came from somewhere deep, but also all around. They spread over him and settled, as rain or snow or mist settles in hollows. He spoke the words to himself.

"*Welcome. Take time. More will become clear. Listen.*"

Now he began to hear sounds which were not just of the mountain but of its inhabitants. He heard the nesting and feeding noises of its winged community, the tread, the scratch, the breathing even of its earthbound population. Sounds that told him if it was day or night, a time of growth or of hibernation. And then a different set of noises, out of place yet familiar. The crunching of gravel, the squelch and suck of mud, metallic clicks of metal on stone, rhythmic breathing or rapid panting – and voices saying words he could hear from outside himself now. Banal words, but sending echoes of familiarity.

"*Come on, can't keep stopping.*"
"*Get the map out and check.*"
"*Why couldn't he come?*"
"*Is there a trig point?*"
"*Take a bearing – better be safe.*"
"*Hey – pick that up!*"
"*This meant to be fun?*"
"*So, how's your first Munro then?*"
"*You always have this in mind for your last Munro?*"

As he had learned to differentiate the sounds of birds and animals, even the tiniest of them, so he listened to the variations of this other species. He heard the chatterers, the complainers, the slow and steady, the stop and starters. He identified the groups, the pairs, the stragglers – the loners. He felt how some could work with the surfaces and angles of the mountain, moving smoothly and leaving little trace, while others seemed to fight them, starting little avalanches of scree or stumbling through heather. Once in a while he sensed a powerful despair. Mostly it came and went unchanged. Sometimes it lessened as the ascent continued. But more than once it increased until it was suddenly replaced by an unsettling nothingness and, again, that sense of something unidentified dying.

The sounds mostly headed upwards then downwards, but some seemed to follow the paths of other creatures. These sound trails stopped and started more irregularly. Instead of steady tread and open voices he heard rustling movement close to the very surface of the mountain, urgent whispers followed by silences. Instead of breath exhaled naturally, in time with movement, he heard it held, let out slowly, held again. He would recognise conflicting sensations: excitement and fear, frustration and relief, or exultation and the sense of death.

Time synthesised further. The mountain's past seeped into him and now he roamed not just across and through its mass but back into its life, its store of memories. Memories held not just in time but in place, linked to the mountainscape itself.

At the foot of a cleft that split a near-vertical cliff he encountered both youth and experience.

"*On your long vac then?*"
"*Yes, sir. Came up to join the family at the lodge for a few weeks.*"
"*Good man. Done a bit of climbing then?*"
"*A bit of scrambling in the Lakes. But some chaps are going to the*

Alps and they want me to go with them. Thought I'd get a bit of training. Try a few bigger routes."

"Damned good training too. Don't underestimate these crags. Might not be as high as the Alps but tricky enough, especially in this weather."

"You've been in the Alps I believe, sir. I heard that you were on that first ascent of the Matterhorn, with Mr Whymper. Wasn't that marvellous, being the first ever to stand on such a top?"

"Nearly fifty years ago that was. 1865. Bad memories though. Four fellows killed and lucky to get down myself. Taken me a while but one thing I've learned – don't have to get to the top to appreciate a mountain. But probably too early to give you that advice. It's summits you're thinking about. Course it is. People used to avoid the high places because they seemed wild, dangerous. Nowadays that's what seems to attract us. So you look after yourself, young lad. Wonderful things mountains – but don't turn your back on them, take my meaning? Where's your father though? He's usually keen to recapture a bit of lost youth."

"He was called back to London last night. Something about Sarajevo, wherever that is. Can't imagine it's worth dragging him away."

On a rocky outcrop below the summit he heard both excitement and distaste.

"My God, it's magnificent. I've never seen anything like it. Such grandeur. These chasms, they turn one giddy. And look, Brown, how that mist steams around the summit and mingles with the clouds themselves."

"Yes indeed, very fine I suppose for you poets and your romantic dispositions, but I observe no inn or any other human habitation. You see some sort of magnificence where I look on a landscape fit only for savages. Come man, we must think of our civilised comforts. We cannot feed on these scenes."

"You are a philistine, my friend. I could find sustenance here to sate every sense. Beauty is Truth indeed, and I have rarely seen a *more truthful vista. See man, the veils of cloud now open and show the mountain as if through a celestial loophole. And now that loophole widens, revealing fresh prospects both far and near!"*

"A mutton pie and some ale would also be a fine prospect."

Around and inside the rectangular remnants of a shieling he listened to the sound of mother and children.

"Alasdair! Angus! Awae an creel in mair peats. Yir faither hasnae left near eneuch. Gae on noo, nor we'll freeze the nicht. An tak tent o the beasts. Mind they dinnae stravaig ower muckle."

"Hoo couldnae faither bide here?"

"Ach, Alasdair, ye ken fine aw the men maun gang doon tae the glen an see tae the hairst wi the kye here oot the wey. Whiniver that's done wae we'll aw gang doon an yir faither'll tak the kye tae merkit. Atween hauns ye maun be the man up here. Jist keek at yir sisters – workin awae tae mak cheese an butter tae tak doon. So haud yir wheesht aboot yir faither."

"Aye, but did ye no see Iseabail rin awae, wae you doon at the burn? Haudin hauns wae that Donald. It's no jist butter an cheese that she's makin."

Near the foot of the mountain the memory held a tale from long past, a tale distilled from fear and superstition.

"Who made the mountains? A good question, child. A high mountain like this would be the work of the Caiileach. Some believe she would stride across the land with her creels of rocks and those she dropped made the hills and mountains. Others say she built the mountains, for stepping stones. She would use hammers to shape the hills and the valleys to her purpose. But we must beware her, for she brings the cold and snow that turns the world to stone."

"But it's summer now gran, so can I go up to the bit where you can pick the cloudberries?"

"Up there on your own? Indeed you cannot – the Daoine Shith

would just love to find a wee girl like you."

"Who, gran?"

"The elfin people, my love. The 'men of peace' as we call them for their silent ways. They can move with no more sound than a gust of wind, like the swishing of a sword drawn through air. You know that strangeness when there comes a sudden whirl of wind on a calm day? That's the Daoine Shith travelling together."

"Are they wicked?"

"They are not wicked, but they envy mankind and will steal wee babies if they're not baptised in time. When you were born we hammered nails into the board of the bed. That keeps them off. So no more of your wandering off alone. Down here is safe for you."

Chapter after chapter spoke its story until the store of memories faded and faded further and there was just the mountain and one silent remembrance of its own far past. A remembrance of a great crushing weight upon it, a weight that hardly seemed to move but still scraped and scoured and grated and ground, and altered the mountain forever. At the end of this last tunnel of time there was nothing, just blankness. Nowhere further to explore. And so he returned.

On the surface of the mountain he felt, then heard, two figures climb slowly. They stopped, looked around them, then decided.

The Cailleach

"This high enough for the view then? But not too high, eh?"

"Yeah, we'd better pay attention to that sheet we got. What does it say? 'Avoid mountain tops. They tend to be acidic areas and the phosphates and calcium will over-stimulate plant growth, upsetting the natural ecology.' So it says."

"You mean he'd be pushin' up daisies?"

"Behave. A bit of dignity here. Come on, let's give him his send off. He'll be at home here if anywhere. Then get that dram out."

He felt the grey powder as it was scattered. Time passed. Ash melded into mountain, and he whispered:

"Welcome. Take time. More will become clear. Listen."

The Good Companion

Everyone who likes to go walking knows that it's important to have the right companion, or companions. Being well-matched in pace, for instance, is helpful. But for years I've been walking with someone who, if I'm honest, has a number of faults. For a start he's an aristocratic type. Not that you'd always know it, but he's got what those who bother about those things call 'breeding'. However, the real problem I have is that, even though he's smaller than me, and often untidy-looking, he still seems to attract any women we meet. Attract them to the extent that they will often run their fingers through his luxuriant hair, comment on how gorgeous he is – and then feed him a biscuit. Not once has that happened to me. Well there was that time that…but that's another story. So there you go, that's what happens when you go walking with a West Highland Terrier.

I'm also jealous of his name – Cuillin. One reason is obvious: as a walker I wish that I too had been named after a mountain range, and the finest set of mountains in Britain come to that. I mean, Torridon Laing sounds pretty cool, even Drumochter Laing. (Though I might have drawn the line at Campsie Fells Laing.)

But his name is even better than that: according to mythology it derives from Cú Chulainn, an Irish hero renowned for his terrifying battle frenzy. And just to make things perfect this hero was known as the 'Hound of Ulster'. How great is that?

All of this etymological material may be giving you the idea of some sort of noble canine companion, loping along beside me as I stride out, a dog whose eyes are on the far horizons, his thoughts filled with images of paw-to-paw combat with any dog which steps in his way. Forget it. This dog is less like a hero of the battle and more like the Scottish army camp followers, appropriately known as 'the sma' folk', who emerge after the combat, searching the corpses for anything of value. Anyone walking with him must endure a mixture of admiration and frustration as his nose, rarely more than an inch off the ground, assists him in his pursuit of food of any kind. If Cuillin were a human running a 10K or half-marathon this is how his race would go. When the gun fired he would watch as the field streamed away, preferring to wander around for a few minutes taking in the smells of embrocation left by the other competitors. After a while he would look up, sprint after the rest, but then stop again to investigate a few of the vans selling burgers or pizza. And so it would go on: sprint, stop, trot, wander off-course, sprint, stop to give himself a good scratch, trot, chat to spectators who might be carrying food. And on finally crossing the line he would expect extravagant praise and perhaps a couple of biscuits with his re-hydrating water. Obviously a strange way for an athlete to run but for Cuillin a kind of enjoyable canine fartlek.

Walking, it is well known, helps the thinking process; it stimulates the imagination. Many famous authors were long-distance walkers who sought inspiration from their peregrinations, and who also loved dogs. Dickens regularly walked twenty or thirty miles, often through the night. Such was his obsessiveness that he claimed: 'If I couldn't walk fast and far I should just explode and perish.' He liked large dogs such as Newfoundlands and Mastiffs, and of course wrote a splendid canine character in the fearsome shape of Bill Sykes' Bullseye. Wordsworth is said to have walked tens of thousands of miles in his lifetime, and as he walked he would try out his poems on his accompanying dogs. Perhaps a case for the

RSPCA. Coleridge was also a prodigious pedestrian, once walking ninety miles across Exmoor and back in two days. His love of dogs was encapsulated in this quotation: 'The one absolutely unselfish friend that man can have in this selfish world, the one that never deserts him, the one that never proves ungrateful or treacherous, is his dog.'

But what if those literary giants had had a West Highland as a companion on those long inspirational walks? Instead of that prodigious output of novels and articles I guarantee that Dickens would not have written more than a few short stories and perhaps an unfinished novella – assuming he hadn't 'exploded' before even that. To the relief of thousands of school-pupils Coleridge's *Ancient Mariner*, inspired while on a walking tour with William and Dorothy Wordsworth, plus dogs, might have come to a stop before that symbolic albatross was even spotted, thus saving everyone approximately 135 verses. Wordsworth himself, if constantly dragging a terrier out of the daffodils, would never have got close to his near-four-hundred poem output. All very well to be wandering *'lonely as a cloud'* thinking fine thoughts but if you're wandering along checking where that sodding dog has got to this time your thoughts become less poetic.

The walks I take with Cuillin are shorter. One of the favourites is through the Quarrymill Woodland Walk, on the edge of Scone. This walk has everything. There is the starting point, used by so many dogs that the first twenty metres are clearly a kind of sniff-nirvana to the connoisseur

Fido! I wandered lonely as a cloud.

of canine smells. Apparently the area of a dog's brain devoted to analysing scent is forty times greater than that of the human. They have around 220 million olfactory receptors in their noses. Sometimes they seem to be using them one by one. Once the walk has begun properly there is the Annaty Burn to investigate. When Cuillin was younger, the bankings were for racing up and down for the sheer joy of it. With the onset of intermittent maturity this behaviour is now reserved for a couple of downhill sections of path. There are ducks to either ignore or terrify depending on the mood – and of course, where there are ducks there is the possibility of bread. Another attraction linked to food is the sighting of a mobility scooter on the well-maintained paths. We used to meet a man who kept a box of dog treats on his scooter. All the local dogs knew him. But I'm not convinced that every dog then expressed the Pavlovian response of chasing every mobility scooter in the expectation of biscuits.

Suddenly stick-chasing lost its appeal to Cuillin.

Quarrymill, however, could also bring excitement and danger. One winter I had to break the thin covering of ice on the Quarrymill pond and wade towards a terrified Cuillin, who had changed in one scrabbling instant from, 'Hey, look at me walking on this cool shiny-white stuff' to 'Help, why have I fallen through the ground into this freezing water and why can't I pull myself out and who's going to rescue me?' The rescue was duly effected, confirming, if any confirmation were needed, that denim jeans in water are on a par with open-toed sandals in the snow.

However, as I am frequently reminded of by people who clearly regard me as some kind of hermit risk, 'he gets you out of the house.' Indeed he does. When I'm sitting with a good book on one side, a cup of coffee on the other, idly contemplating whether the right term for what's hitting the window is tippling down, pelting, raining cats and dogs, or whether the snow can be categorised as dry drift, smore drift, or yowdendrift – he does indeed get you out of the house. In such weather, which would allow my human walking companions to shake their heads ruefully and agree that walking would be out of the question and the only alternative is the pub…he gets you out of the house. He takes the cliché 'There's no bad weather, just wrong clothes' and shortens it to 'There's no bad weather.' I suppose I should admire his ability to go out without a protective shield of Gore-Tex, to roll around in the snow like some hardy, slightly-insane Scandinavian enjoying the ritual of the sauna, or plouter about in any convenient bit of water, emerging to make his head even more convenient to pat by placing sopping paws on my thighs.

The problem is that these frankly exhibitionist displays are enacted while I stand passively, rain or snow dripping or accumulating on me. And once he's decided that this particular fun is over and we can walk on, what happens? We meet another dog and more rituals must be observed. I stand, exchanging a few platitudes about the weather with the owner, while the dogs forget entirely about making progress in their respective walks in the exciting mystery of sniff-analysis. Depending on the results of this process they may move on to running round in circles, advanced lead-tangling – or may decide to trot on.

When I walk in the hills with human companions and we meet other walkers communication is usually limited to a 'Fine day' if so it is, but more likely a shake of the head and a raising of the eyebrows to acknowledge the idiocy of being out in this weather. Absolutely no sniffing occurs.

Another canine/human comparison involves food for the journey. I have never walked with any person who encourages me to share my chocolate, orange, or soup by stopping to stare at me or pawing my leg. To be honest, if that did happen I would be unlikely to walk with that person again. Even when offered food by a friend the usual response of hill-walkers is 'No, I'm fine' or 'Got some myself, thanks.' It's a kind of unwritten code unrecognised by my dog. In his mind I am clearly a kind of Sherpa: delivering him to the start of the walk, opening gates for him, and above all carrying his provisions and delivering them on demand.

When in Scone Park other Sherpas/dog-walkers, I notice, encourage more energetic exercise by throwing balls, often using these extra-arm sling affairs which permit the user to launch the ball further than trained cricketers. A bit like ballistas – and sometimes referred to as 'weapons of mass exhaustion'. The dog races after the ball, races back, deposits it and waits for the process to repeat. Excellent. Except that Cuillin regards chasing balls with friendly curiosity but absolutely no interest in participation. I have tried it a few times and his attitude is quite clear: 'Interesting. My member of staff has thrown this round object away. I presume he doesn't want it. I'm not surprised since it doesn't smell edible. Now he's pointing at it and getting quite excited. Must be pleased to have got rid of it. Perhaps he could calm down and we could continue our stroll.'

Yes, I know. There are dogs who allow their owners to walk at a brisk and regular pace, dogs who walk to heel, dogs who happily and repetitively chase balls, dogs who never ask for food. Perhaps they lack the independent spirit of my particular walking companion. Perhaps I should blame his pedigree status, making him highly strung. Or perhaps, as is so often the case, I should blame his human parents. Excuse me, I have to stop writing now. He wants his walk.

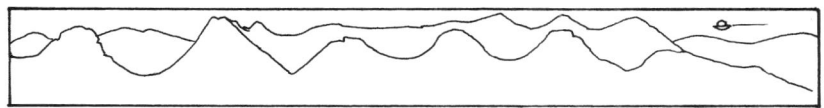

ALIEN IN ETIVE

*'Mork to planet Zog.
Earth time 1:00 am.
Earth coordinates NN 158 507.
Status Report:'*

I SUCCESSFULLY INTERCEPTED my observation group today, later than anticipated due to problems with my spatial gears near a place called 'The Green Welly Stop' at Tyndrum. (No information found regarding significance of 'The Green Welly' in Earth culture.) Coordinates finally brought me to a small, primitively-constructed building in a wilderness area they call 'Glen Etive'. From my Earth camouflage options I selected *Musca domestica* (more commonly referred to by subjects as the 'house-fly'), tele-formed myself, and entered.

I needed to use auxiliary breathing equipment as my air pollution meter was clicking just below 'noxious', showing high levels of perspiration and alcohol fumes. This was difficult to understand as air outside registered 'pure'. First indications were that this was some kind of prison or punishment cell. The subjects – twelve in total, and all of the same Earth gender – were crowded together on a single raised platform, not the soft, individual bases reported elsewhere. The subjects were in the standby mode they refer to as 'sleeping' yet many seemed to continue to communicate, emitting irregular sound patterns. Unfortunately my translation device failed to recognise anything linguistically intelligible.

The subjects were all encased in the kind of soft carapace from which we have seen Earth insects emerge in colourful and often attractive form. As the light sector approached I looked forward to seeing such a transformation, but I must report that, as they exited, these creatures surely could not be classified as aesthetically pleasing in any universe with which we are familiar.

The subjects were all encased in a soft carapace.

Further evidence that they may be prisoners of some kind is that their names are printed on their clothing, presumably for purposes of identification: Berghaus, Páramo, Rab, Mountain Equipment. Several are labelled Gore-Tex and I deduce they are either from the same unit they call 'family' or perhaps the kind of anti-social unit they term 'gang'. There did not appear to be any subjects operating as guards of any kind and, since evidence so far suggested that the subjects must have been placed here against their wishes, it seemed that they are under surveillance by a system more advanced than the primitive image collectors reported in urban areas.

'Earth time 7:00 am.'

Further evidence they might be prisoners.

Observing their slow-motion movements when they moved from their standby mode area it was clear that their physiological booting up systems were underpowered. After they prepared and ingested various types of fuel (see separate report) communication increased and preparations were made involving the filling of large sacks of brightly-coloured material. These could then be attached to the subject using a system of harness. They then exited their building and began to walk, still attached to their burdens. Furthermore, they made no attempt to access any of the vehicles stationed outside the building, again suggesting their lack of privileges. Their movements were slow and clumsy, many of the creatures utilising simple balancing devices, twin poles held in the hand and placed on the ground with each leg movement. I must report my astonishment at this exceptionally primitive method of moving materials. Clearly teleporting has either not been invented here or is denied to these subjects as a form of punishment.

Once out of the building I changed my camouflage option to *Lepus timidus*, usually referred to here by the term, 'mountain hare'. (As we have discovered, Earth creatures not only reduce their efficiency by the use multiple linguistic systems, they also utilise linguistic systems no longer understood by 99.9% of their society.) Precipitation outside was in the upper scale and there was a danger of operational damage to my wings. The *Lepus timidus* was identified as better suited to my current environment.

For the next period of time there was little to report apart from environmental information (see separate report). My observation group moved slowly along the side of a water-source, across a simple structure, then upwards towards a high point in the environment. As I followed I tried to ascertain their purpose, expecting the efforts they were clearly expending to result in their arrival at a place of some value to them. Their navigational skills seemed extremely limited as they frequently halted, looking around in a confused way and pointing in different directions. Several even pointed at me, still in my *Lepus timidus* form, with great enthusiasm.

At this point one of them brought out what has been identified as a simple navigational aid called a 'map', encased

The group move slowly along the side of a water source, then across a simple structure.

in transparent material. After gazing at it for some time he removed it from its case and unfolded it, causing it to become functionally unstable and in danger of destruction by the air flow. He then placed it on the ground and the subjects stared at it for some time, alternately placing digits on it and pointing upwards. Then one subject, clearly more intelligent, or simply allowed more efficient equipment, brought out a device which sat in his palm. He operated it, and pointed in what I had already computed to be the high point of the environment. At this the amusing expanding 'map' was, with even more amusing difficulty, brought back to its original size, re-encased, and the group moved on.

By this time the precipitation level had increased to a level which rendered their garments relatively inefficient, yet they were clearly unable to deploy any kind of personal protection shield. Perhaps this was another element of what was still

He brought out a small flat object functionally unstable in danger of destruction by the air flow.

appearing to be their punishment. They cannot have been allowed to return to the security of their building, presumably aware that their movements were being monitored. Continuing upwards they approached the high point, and I was interested to see what drew them there. They could not have been there for observation purposes as the cooling air changed from invisible gas to the miniature water droplets they call 'mist', rendering visibility extremely limited. To my surprise (though nothing should surprise us further regarding this strange world) they arrived at a pyramid shaped pile of small stones which seemed of little value or use. Perhaps, I surmised, there was some kind of religious significance attached to the strange structure.

A few of the subjects did touch the stone shape, and two added further stones, but if this was some kind of ceremonial rite the others did not participate. Then, to my surprise, they appeared to ready themselves to descend. Had they expended

The summit pile. Perhaps there was religious significance.

this effort simply for this? As an experiment I approached in my *Lepus* form and began to assemble a small stone pyramid of my own. The effect of this simple activity was highly significant. The group became extremely excited, bringing out hand-held devices which I have confirmed to be capable of image capture. They approached very cautiously so I tested their reactions further by placing one forelimb to my head and one to my chest, in imitation of the ceremonial gestures which have been recorded elsewhere. The group's astonishment levels were now raised to what I considered to be dangerous levels, so I retreated and observed from a distance.

In time the excitement level dropped and I waited to see what might be a more practical reason for their presence there. To my disappointment all that happened now, apart from an assault on my *Lepus timidus* form by another sexually active, ironically named *Lepus timidus*, was a descent back to their dwelling. This was again a journey of considerable effort to the subjects. By this time many were making extensive use of the metallic poles referred to above. The entire activity had had no purpose which I could discern, and my only theory remains my original one: that they are somehow being monitored and forced to behave in this manner as a punishment. The alternative, that they do this for pleasurable reasons, seems unlikely in the extreme.

'*Report terminates.*'

"I sentence you to 30 years hard hill-walking."

You'll Never Walk Alone

Yes Garry, the guys need to walk as a team.
Just a matter of taking one section at a time.
We know we've not been walking
As well as we're capable of.
The boys up front have been slow,
Not firing on all cylinders.
The back four, to be honest,
Are letting everything past them.
They've all lost a yard of pace.
But we know we're better than that,
We just need to walk in the right areas.

      *   *   *   *

Gutted, Garry? Course we are.
To be fair to the lads though,
A lot were carrying injuries.
Dodgy knees, stiff joints,
Some were carrying hangovers.
The turning point, Garry?
Had to be that disputed bealach.
All downhill after that.
So yeah, walk of two halves.
But at the end of the day -
You just go back to the pub.

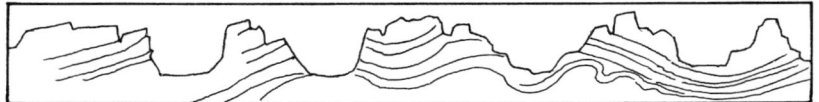

The Pale Mountains

ONE...TWO...THREE...GO! Two fists shot from behind backs, two fingers extended from each fist. And that was it – one finger for the French Alps, two for the Italian Dolomites. Not, perhaps, the way Bonington planned expeditions: 'OK guys. One finger for Everest, two for Changabang.' But encouragingly, our first decision was unanimous and the Laing-Brown Trans-Dolomite trek was up and, if not yet running, at least on the starting line. We were a well-matched team. Martin: ex-Mountain Rescue, excellent navigator, organised and competent, whippet-lean. Myself: accident-prone, capable of getting lost in a lift, two years from my state pension. It was like a combination of Bear Grylls and Mr Bean. But we had hill walked and Munro bagged together for years, without problem. Now it was time to go European.

Armed with the excellent *Cicerone Guide* we selected the *Alta Via 2* route from Bressanone in the north to Feltre in the south, a route covering a modest hundred miles but approximately 10,000 metres of ascent and similar descent figures. There would be some vie ferrate – cable-assisted climbing – on the way, but nothing very technical. At the end of each section we would have a pre-booked rifugio, mostly at 2,000 metres or more. A rifugio is exactly like the average Scottish bothy – if the bothy were warm and clean, contained anything up to 90 beds, served dinner and breakfast and sold beer, wine and other alcoholic refreshments. If Carlsberg did bothies...

If Carlsberg did bothies...

Now, a warning. If you want a useful and practical section by section guide to the AV2 my advice is to stop reading here and turn to the *Cicerone Guide*. Its first sentence, by the way, is '*Mountain walking can be a dangerous activity carrying a risk of personal injury or death.*' I always think that 'death' is a good word for getting your attention; maybe it should always be in italics, followed by several exclamation marks...and perhaps underlined. This account will be both rambling and impressionistic, a bit like wandering through the Quirang in the mist. So no boring details about what to pack, what maps to take, the journey to our Bressanone starting point.

The first section of the route was short and straightforward, leading us up 1,900 metres and face-to-face with our first close-up of this magical mountainscape. The reason it was short was due to our sensible willingness to take advice from the guidebook. It stated that, '*non-purists will appreciate the buses and lift to ease the 1900m height gain.*' An early dilemma. Were we 'purists'? Or merely pragmatic Scots with healthily under-developed Protestant ethics? Would we, for example, drive to the Cairngorm car park, or insist on walking up to it? Did we accept that the local economy would benefit from our sensible use of the transport infrastructure? Look out – here comes the cable car.

I suppose I should try to give some sort of idea of what we saw on that first day. From the terrace of Rifugio Città di Bressanone we looked across green pasture, a belt of forest... then a serrated, shark's maw ridge which seemed part natural, part CGI. Imagine the Cuillin ridge on Skye had Donald Trump been into landscape design. It was too early in the day for the full orangey-pink 'enrosadira' effect, but the giant, knuckled fist of a ridge still glowed against a flawless blue backdrop. Huge scree slopes poured down from the knifed-out gullies above, looking from this distance more like fine sand than chunks of rock. The legend of the Dolomites is that the rock surface is covered in fine white gossamer woven from moon rays, to remind a princess bride of the lunar landscapes of her homeland. Eighteenth century geologist Déodat de Dolomieu, after whom the mountains were renamed from the original *Pale Mountains*, offered a different, more scientific explanation, but I'm going with the princess.

If the first day was easy the second one first lulled us with a pleasant woodland meander then hit us with a kidney punch. Let's examine the route the AV2 takes through the Dolomites. Imagine a sheet of corrugated iron, whitish-grey rather than rusty red. Now imagine that you are an ant. What's the sensible way to traverse it? Along one of the runnels of course, like strolling through a valley. (Of course ants can stroll.) Or, you could travel up and down, over every corrugation, pulling your ant-body upwards then plunging down to repeat the process. The good news is that there's a little ant rifugio near the top of most of the corrugations, to provide food, a rest and a view before descending again. So, like little worker ants, we climb, in baking heat, up a path of blinding white limestone, towards Forcella di Putia at nearly two and a half thousand metres. Despite the skeleton dryness of the stones underfoot the path is dotted by survivalist alpines, seemingly existing on a diet of fresh air and optimism. Trudging upwards, bent over, sweat dripping, I look down at a fragile, acrylic-blue, Trumpet Gentian pointing its petals towards me and seeming to whisper, 'Get your size seven boots away from me, you clumsy Scotsman.' But eventually the saddle is mounted, rock transforms into grassy slopes and Rifugio Genova is reached, the second in the series of stunningly situated rifugi which we would encounter on our route.

What was the attraction, then, of this and other similar days? Thankfully, many factors. In Scotland, Martin and I would 'visit' mountains, getting to the top, looking around at the fine view of mist, then descend to the car, bunkhouse, pub, whatever. Here, because of the rifugio system, we 'inhabited' the mountain environment, the more so as we walked further into the heart of what Le Corbusier famously called, 'the most beautiful work of architecture ever created.' Surrounded by these dramatic walls of rock we walked, ate, slept and woke up in the Dolomites…then did it again, and again. Repetitive? Yes, as all walking can be. But never monotonous. The film set quality of the Dolomites, their sense of 'otherness', took care of that.

Another factor which separated this experience from Munro bashing was the chance to meet others on the route. Since those others were doing part or the whole of this Alta Via we started to get to know fellow pilgrims who started at the same time as us. They ranged widely in nationality: Austrian, German, Swedish, Norwegian, French – and Mark from Belgium, who later turned our duo into a trio. By the end of the fifth stage Martin was organising one long dinner table for this European Union of trekkers. The other unifying factor round that table was professional background. Two business consultants, two research doctors, a professor of physics, an SQA administrator, a retired teacher, a social worker, plus two students. I'm not sure what that indicated. Obviously you don't have to be middle class to be attracted to mountains. The Creag Dhu Climbing Club, which led the field in Scottish mountaineering after World War II, was full of working class guys, many from the Glasgow shipyards. More likely is that you need a certain amount of money and relatively flexible holidays to be able to embark on this kind of extended trip. So have we in some way gone back to the era of the 'gentleman' walker? Or 'gentlewoman', since at least the gender balance is now even.

Yet another attraction was the system of vie ferrate, the 'iron roads'. These stretches, offering aid by cables, pitons, metal staples, ladders and such like, added greatly to the sense of doing more than just a Scottish hill walk. On the AV2 they were not of the exacting nature which required equipment other than a good grip and an average head for heights. But they added spice to the relatively plainer fare of straightforward walking. Often they took us up the edges of gullies full of scree debris which, we found out, was liable to act as a highly efficient stone escalator – always going down. So, could Scotland develop this kind of system beyond the recently opened Via Ferrata of Kinlochleven? And add the signposts found wherever paths diverged? Or even the painted route markers keeping walkers on the straight and narrow? It must be a cultural thing. It was clear that continental trekkers were every bit as much lovers of mountains as ourselves. But it is still difficult to imagine painted markers along the Skye Ridge leading to cables and pitons taking one up then down the Inaccessible Pinnacle. Just writing that sentence I hear splutterings, even gasps of imminent cardiac arrest, from the traditionalists. But the new generation of Scottish walkers? I think they would just say, 'bring it on'.

The vie ferrate, however, were also a stark reminder of the darker history of the Dolomites, as were many of the paths we took. During the First World War, far from the trenches of the Western Front, murderous fighting was taking place in these mountains, between the Austro-Hungarian Empire and Italy. Both sides constructed mule tracks to facilitate the movement of supplies – tracks we now walked on. Both sides fashioned the 'iron roads' to allow men and supplies to reach and defend important but inaccessible places. So where we saw the highest concentration of ladders, cables and pitons it was likely to have been an area of the fiercest fighting. The men in both armies existed in terrible conditions, with the cold and avalanches killing more than died in actual combat. In response to this, inside the massive bulk of Marmolada – at 3,342 metres the highest peak in the Dolomites – the Austrians constructed a 'City of Ice' for shelter, with twelve kilometres of tunnels running through its interior.

So, as we walked through this quiet, peaceful scenery, we would come across the detritus of war, such as the remains of fortifications, trenches and tunnels. Even today the melting of glaciers can reveal not only military equipment but previously interred bodies of soldiers. In 2012 two were found at a height of over 3,000 metres. It was hard not to think of the scattering of yellow and orange Rhaetian poppies as the poignant equivalent of those of Flanders Fields and to see in the mind's eye the caves and trenches filled with men fighting both the opposing forces and the iron cold of winter. Inside Marmolada today can be heard the groans of ice on rock, groans which might seem to echo the suffering of the wounded and dying from a century ago.

As the sections rolled by we were increasingly aware of the geometry of the landscape. There was of course a predominance of the vertical, in the shape of towering cliffs, pinnacles, campanile towers, paths heading straight upwards and downwards. Cutting at right angles along the feet of jagged verticals, like the x-axes of graphs, were more user-friendly paths. They went up, along, or formed angular switchbacks – the Dolomites didn't seem to like curves. Even human contributions followed this pattern in the shape of simple rectangular buildings or cable car routes rising vertically. On the rare occasions when we came across standing water we half expected it to be in the shape of a rectangular swimming pool.

Variety came, however, in a range of separate landscape forms: sections of lunar like landscape; huge quarry style enclosures which would have provided perfect sets for the early *Dr Who* or *Star Trek* programmes; smaller areas of pillars and pinnacles – rocky chapels inside the overarching Dolomite cathedral; open stretches studded with formations reminiscent of the sandstone buttes in John Ford's images of Monument Valley. Then there were the *Wizard of Oz* moments. As we descended, the Kansas monochromes turned to a technicolour Land of Oz, trees and meadows illuminated by orange lilies, poppies, alpenrose, anemone... In Scotland we probably take colour for granted. Yes, we can spend part of a hill walking day surrounded by rock and scree. But at some point we inevitably return to trees, grass, heather. Walking *in* mountains, rather than up and down them, meant that after several days at height the return to lushness and colour was all the more striking.

And what about the bird and animal life? It was very similar to Scotland. By that I mean the projected *image* of lands teeming with wildlife. We have become used to material aimed at attracting tourists to Scotland, showing golden eagles, capercaillie, dolphins, pine martens... In the Dolomites, we read that we might meet ibex, marmots, badgers, salamanders – even brown bears. Marmots were apparently in great supply: cute marmots, furry marmots, even 'romping' marmots! Now, no doubt, with sufficient time, local knowledge, patience, visitors to Scotland and to the Dolomites *might* encounter those creatures. It must be admitted however that, over two weeks, our wildlife sightings were limited to dozens of Alpine choughs and a couple of buzzards. To be fair, we did finally sight a marmot. Stuffed. In the Natural History Museum, Verona. And it sure wasn't romping. It's another dilemma: should tourist boards feed us advertisement style visions unlikely to be fulfilled, or honest assessments of what is likely to be seen over a short period? What is more important: extra numbers of expectant tourists or the risk of those tourists feeling short-changed by the lack of dolphins waving flippers to them from Scottish waters, golden eagles offering photo opportunities by swooping down to pose on nearby branches?

However, were we overly disappointed by this dearth of frolicking wildlife? Of course not. We're Scottish. Nor did we necessarily believe the wildlife hype we read in advance. In some ways the very emptiness of the surroundings – frequently there were no other humans in sight, far less wildlife – added to that sense of being not just in another country but on another planet. A planet on which travelling life reduced itself to a few simplicities to be considered each day: how far, how high, how far down? To quote Robert Macfarlane:

'One forgets that there are environments which do not respond to the flick of a switch or the twist of a dial, and which have their own rhythms and orders of existence.' [1]

If two elements were to be selected from our trip one would be the sense of the Dolomites as a work of landscape art. The other would be our temporary existence in a place of day to day simplicity; repetitive, yes, but its rhythm and order absolutely,

---

[1] Robert Macfarlane, *Mountains of the Mind: Adventures in Reaching the Summit* (2004)

totally rewarding. Forget the contemporary travel guides which try to lure tourists to this or that area. One of the first guidebooks to be published specifically aimed at travellers and explorers was John Murray's handbook, which came out in 1837. In it he sums up those Pale Mountains:

> *'They are unlike any other mountains, and are to be seen nowhere else among the Alps. They arrest the attention by the singularity and picturesqueness of their forms, by their sharp peaks or horns, sometimes rising up in pinnacles and obelisks, at others extending in serrated ridges, teethed like the jaw of an alligator.'*

One hundred and eighty years later they have not changed.

SIDEWALK RAGE

So, WHAT'S NEW YORK FAMOUS FOR? Central Park? The Empire State Building? Times Square? Of course, but it's also famous for something more prosaic. It's famous for – walking. In this busy city, home to flotillas of yellow taxis and 370 kilometres of subway line, people walk further and faster than in any other American city. I spent five days there recently, walking everywhere, if possible, and it was like being in an outdoor gymnasium, walking a treadmill with the speed cranked up to 'watch you don't fall off, buddy'.

If only I came from Glasgow.

Now, when I say people walk quickly here I mean native New Yorkers, not the ambling, rubber-necking, stop-start tourists who clog up the downtown area.[2] These out-of-towners are public enemies whose walking habits are lambasted in a variety of newspaper articles and blogging sites, which declare:

> *'If you need to break the flow of traffic to do anything, step off to the goddamn side,'* or *'If you and your friends take up the entire crowded sidewalk...I'll be hoping for an errant cab to clip the person on the end.'*

Another blogger declared that most New Yorkers frequently *'felt the need to shoulder a meandering tourist through a store window'* which is marginally less violent than the citizen who warned that his response to lack of walking etiquette might be *'a punch in the throat.'* Other commentators go for the 'more in sorrow than anger' approach and offer helpful tips on *'How to walk in New York'*. Much of the advice is similar to our *Highway Code* and couched in similar terms, talking of lanes, tail-gating, rear-ending, pedestrian rage. You're advised to walk on the right, walk at the speed of the pedestrian traffic, not stop suddenly, not spread across the sidewalk in a group. One interesting difference, however, between advice for walking and driving refers to 'sidewalk rage'. The suggestion is that inside your car you might feel safe enough to indulge in what we might call digital aggression. In the open air, it is suggested, this might not always be advisable.

Out of interest I googled *'How to walk in London'* and it only covered the kind of places *where* you should walk. It was exactly the same for Paris. Berlin, I thought, might be strong on pedestrian rules and regulations.[3] So I tried *'How to walk in Berlin'* but again the sites were concerned with where and not how. So it was New York which seemed unusually fixated

---

[2] Apologies for stereotyping: Ed.
[3] Apologies for stereotyping: Ed.

on walking etiquette – and expressed that fixation with the typical New York forthrightness exemplified above.

A more light-hearted response to the tourist 'problem' came from a New York City based comedy collective, *'Improv Everywhere'*. They created separate *Tourist/New Yorker* walking lanes by chalking official looking lines down the middle of a Fifth Avenue sidewalk, and pretending to be Department of Transportation employees dressed in Hi-Vis waistcoats, controlling this 'test run' before it was to be rolled out across the city. Many tourists were convinced that this was no prank. Elsewhere, scientists are conducting serious experiments in pedestrian organisation. A quick google reveals: *'Pedestrian-dynamics experiment: lane formation in counter flow'*, *'Uni- and bi-directional pedestrian flow in view-limited conditions'*, and my personal favourite, *'Impact of holding umbrella on uni- and bi-directional pedestrian flow.'*

And you thought walking was simple?

During my own stay in New York I could not afford the exorbitant rates of the central hotels. Instead I found one in Billy Joel territory, away from the tourist traps. Decanting from this hotel onto the street there was the immediate feeling of being in a real neighbourhood and not a holiday destination. Shops sold useful stuff, parents pushed strollers, dogs were being walked – and people walked with purpose and speed. After only a short time as a temporary New Yorker I began to identify with their culture. Navigating the easy to follow grid system I noticed that I was consistently covering a block a minute. I felt that I was walking quickly but I soon learned that this speed was just par for the course. Every now and then I tried to burn off an old lady or a guy with a walking frame but it was like that scene in *Butch Cassidy and the Sundance Kid* where Butch and the Kid just couldn't shake off the pursuing posse. *'Who are those guys?'* I quoted internally.

Perhaps it has always been this way. In Francis Spufford's wonderful novel of eighteenth century New York, *Golden Hill*, he describes what we now call Broadway:

> 'The Broad Way, it turned out, as he leaned and craned from the window, was a species of cobbled avenue, only middling broad, lined on Mrs Lee's side with small trees. Wagon-drivers, hawkers with handcarts and quick-paced pedestrians were passing in both directions.'

Broadway has lost its cobbles, wagons have been replaced by trucks, but the pedestrians are still 'quick-paced', as they are in many large cities. So why is this? In a speech to *The American Psychological Association* Professor Stanley Milgram spoke of *'the sensory overload of the city prompting a social withdrawal response – in this case a rapid motor action – to limit a person's environmental stimulation'*.[4] So, while ordinary citizens speed along in a kind of protective bubble, tourists are happy to get 'environmentally stimulated' to hell! Perhaps it is why walking in parks or woods or hills tends to be more leisurely, as the environment relaxes rather than over-stimulates.

The most impressive pedestrians in my temporary neighbourhood were undoubtedly the mothers, occasionally fathers, in charge of buggies containing babies or small toddlers. Although no actual blades were attached to their wheels they had clearly taken inspiration from Boudica and her apocryphal chariot. Not only did they travel at speed, cutting a swathe through the more defenceless pedestrians, they also took multitasking to new levels. Somehow they managed to combine jogging, talking on their phones, drinking coffee, and in some cases simultaneously walking the dog. If I had peered into any of those buggies I would have expected to see one small hand clutching a tiny phone and another turning the pages of the

---

[4] Stanley Milgram, 'The Experience of Living in Cities', *Science*, 167, 3924 (13 March 1970).

cloth-paged edition of Trump's *The Art of the Deal*.

Nor was speed walking restricted to the outside environment. In what became my favourite local diner I stared in awe as the waiters and waitresses zipped and zoomed from table to table, watched over by a guy who probably carried the title 'coach' rather than 'manager'. I'm sure he also carried a stopwatch. Appropriately, the staff were turned out in a livery of red and white, matching that of the Ferrari pit crew. 'How like home,' I thought. 'Fast, efficient service.'

Meanwhile, downtown, a plan is clearly developing to get some of those idiot tourists off the actual streets. The High Line is a walkway built on an elevated section of a disused railroad spur. Inspired by a similar project in Paris it has been planted out as a kind of linear park. Its height gives a new perspective on the buildings on either side, and allows widescreen views of the Hudson River. When I walked along it, the High Line was clearly doing its job, taking hordes of tourists into a safe and attractive place where, so long as they could walk in a straight line, they were no danger to themselves or to purposeful New Yorkers. It gets nearly five million visitors annually so, one would think, that must empty the streets of those pesky tourists. The problem is, it's only a mile and a half long, so those five million trips don't take much more than half an hour each – maybe an hour if you add on a return journey. Perhaps the plan is to build hundreds of these aerial sidewalks around Manhattan so visitors can stop and start, change direction, halt suddenly to whip out cameras, and annoy no one but themselves. And if they should want to descend to street level, then that would be allowed after passing a short 'fit to walk' assessment.

Of course tourists are not the only problematic pedestrians. There are also the 'petextrians' – people who may not be able to walk and chew gum but think they can navigate crowded streets and intersections while undertaking complicated tasks on their phones. 'Distracted walking' injuries are increasing all over the United States: there have been incidents such as walking off a cliff, into fountains, off railway platforms. And guess what – they are mostly caused by young people. And guess what again – in a survey of eight cities New Yorkers were the most likely to view distracted walking as a serious issue. Not only are New Yorkers themselves undertaking the usual essential tasks on their phones, there is the added factor of those tourists walking along while staring down at their Google Maps, like tech-savvy mice navigating a tricky maze.

I mean, it's dangerous enough at intersections even when fully concentrating. The old *Walk/Don't Walk* lights may have been changed to pictograms of *Walking Person/Warning Hand*, but for New York taxi drivers – and pedestrians – old habits die hard. Like the promises of pre-election politicians, crossing signals are merely advisory. What we would call jaywalking is just 'walking'. If no vehicles are coming, then walk on. Unfortunately car drivers take the same approach, as I found out. If I said that I had a *Midnight Cowboy* moment, some of you may remember that 1969 film when Dustin Hoffman had an unscripted argument with a New York yellow cab. The cameras were rolling as he crossed an intersection and he was nearly run over by a cab jumping the lights. He instinctively banged on its bonnet, shouting, 'I'm walkin' here! I'm walkin' here!' followed by a splendid example of the digital aggression mentioned earlier. This adlib reaction was kept in the film and can still be seen on YouTube. The same thing happened to me. (Although I was not being filmed at the time, was not wearing a white suit, and did not have Jon Voight walking alongside me in a Stetson and fringed jacket.) Walking briskly on the instructions of the *Walking Person* signal I was almost across when I had to leap out of the way of a taxi which came barrelling around the corner. If only I came from Glasgow – I'd have ripped his windscreen wipers off.[5] Having been brought up near Edinburgh I mouthed 'Sorry' and walked on. Maybe, after all, I wouldn't make a real New Yorker.

---

[5] Apologies for stereotyping: Ed.

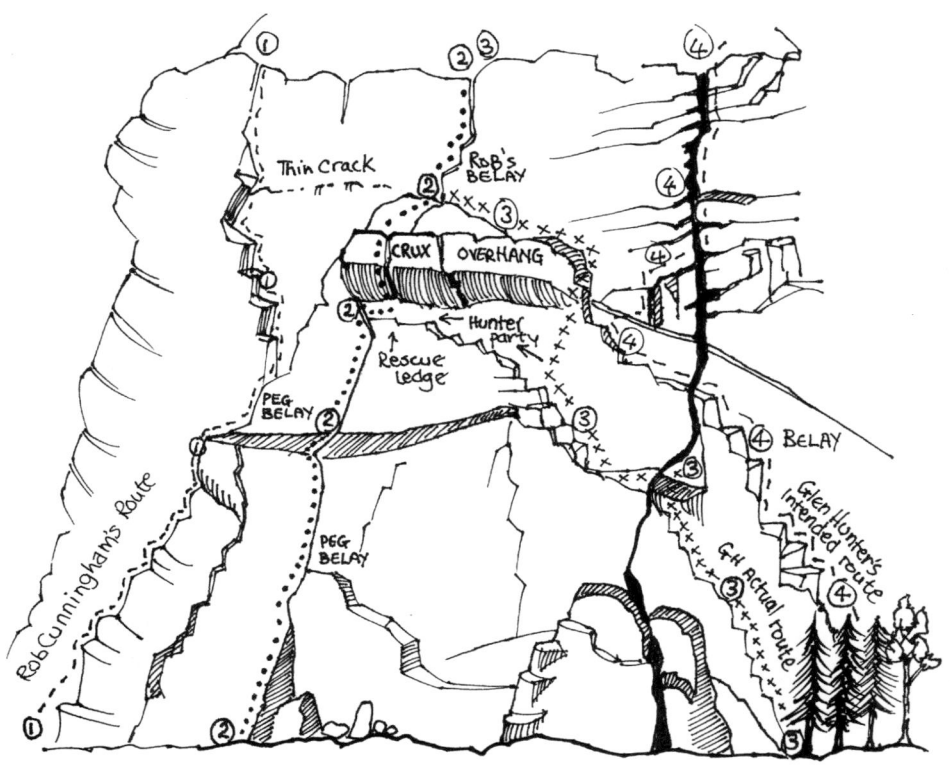

The Buachaille: Central Buttress.

1 Wanderlust – HVS
2 Lusty Crack – Extreme
3 Diagonal Step – Severe
4 Easy Route – V.Diff

'THE ICE-MAN'

DRAMATIC RESCUE ON BUACHAILLE ETIVE MOR.
Climber risks own life to save others

THE SCOTTISH MOUNTAINS saw yet another tragic fatality yesterday. A young climber, Glen Hunter (18), plunged to his death while on a rock climb in Glencoe. However, two other young climbers were saved from almost certain death by the heroic efforts of another climber, who put the safety of others before his own. Rob Cunningham (34), a highly experienced mountaineer from Dunkeld, was on a solo climb on the East buttress of Buachaille Etive Mor when he saw two figures clearly in difficulties above him.

The three – Glen Hunter (18), Peter Doig (19), Ian Wakefield (17) – had been high on a relatively straightforward route up the easier area of the buttress but somehow strayed onto a much more technical parallel climb which brought them below an overhang they could not negotiate. In trying to retreat Glen had lost his grip and fallen several hundred feet to his death. The remaining two, traumatised by the loss of their companion, were now marooned on the face, unable to ascend and too terrified to attempt a further descent. To compound their desperate situation heavy rain started to fall.

Mr Cunningham, who was on a solo ascent of a route some distance from the one they had strayed onto, quickly assessed the situation and decided that descending and calling in Mountain Rescue might well take too long. The young men were shouting to him that they were exhausted and were in danger of slipping from their precarious perch. Disregarding his own safety he first climbed upwards then traversed towards them along a crack described by a climber familiar with the area as 'no more than a scratch on the surface of the rock.' Unable to use any protection for this manoeuvre he must have known that he was literally trusting his life to his own hands.

Calming the two terrified teenagers he quickly established a secure belay to which they were then attached. He expertly combined his own safety rope with their climbing rope and persuaded them to abseil in turn down to safety, before following them. He checked the fallen climber for any signs of life, and covered the clearly dead body. He then walked the two survivors towards the road, where they were met by a Mountain Rescue team who had been alerted by another climber.

The two young men were effusive in their praise. Peter Doig said, 'We could feel ourselves going, our hands were getting that wet and cold. How he got across to us I'll never know; it was like he was Spiderman.' Ian Wakefield added, 'He was just so calm. As soon as he got to us you just knew he'd get us down. We can't thank him enough. We just wish we'd been able to help Glen.'

The leader of the rescue team, Archie Morris, knew Mr Cunningham well.

'Rob was just the kind of guy you need in that kind of situation. We call him Ice-man. Always cool under pressure, never seems to show any emotion – even when he's had to deal with fatalities. And I know he's seen a few. Nothing seems to faze him.'

Perth Crematorium
He hadn't wanted to come, but the parents of the dead boy had written to him and said they hoped he'd attend so they could thank him for saving Glen's friends. And they already knew he

lived not far from Perth – he couldn't make that an excuse. So he made his preparations, preparations as careful and organised as those for a difficult climb. Everything in order, physically and mentally; awareness of what the difficulties would be and the protection he would use; what the techniques would be for the crux on any particularly challenging pitch.

He walked to the open doors of the crematorium chapel, hoping that the unfamiliar dark suit and constricting tie would help him to blend in. Pausing, he ran through his mental safety check. First thing to do was make sure you were sitting away from anybody you actually knew, anybody you'd be expected to speak to. So arrive late and pick your spot – where nobody you knew could just slide in beside you and give you a nudge of recognition. Best to be right at an end near the wall, beside a stranger – better still a group of strangers. Folk who wouldn't necessarily be surprised if your...*susceptibility* started to show. Then concentrate on the job in hand – keeping the right look on, turning the mental key and keeping everything locked down safely. But he could still sense the eyes on him, had seen the looks as he had approached the crematorium entrance, had heard the too-loud whisper, 'That's him. Ice-man Cunningham. He's the one that rescued the other two.' What had possessed Archie to use that stupid name when he spoke to the journalist. He was used to it with his mates, who just said it as a bit of banter, but now the papers had picked it up and it was being used as a neat piece of shorthand, a one-dimensional definition.

OK – always helped to have a look at that sign up at the top right of the place: the green man running somewhere and the big letters, FIRE EXIT. Never were truer words written on a crematorium wall. Black humour, the go-to attitude of the climbing fraternity, worn like a battered helmet. No laughing here though. Smiling was fine, along with a wee shake of the head. Made you look in control, a bit reflective even. Lots of those tricks you could play, and the great thing was you could be playing any of them and still look like you were thinking the right thoughts. Counting the heads in front of you, reading the hymn numbers forwards then backwards, working out the favourite colour to wear (just another joke). It was like the familiar distracting stuff before a potentially dangerous climb. Here too it didn't require anything dramatic, just things that could keep you busy: a whole repertoire of looks, shakes of the head, raisings of the eyebrows, words of recognition – mouthed, not spoken – the tight, down-turned, rueful smiles. In other words all the tells of overwhelming grief which could be mustered by the average Scotsman of his generation.

Here comes the funeral party. There's a good juxtaposition for you, the funeral party. Right, 'climbing now'. Start concentrating. Eyes down, laser that hymn book till they're past. Don't look up. Don't look up. Dangerous if some of them are breaking up already – that would be all it would take for him to start having the problems. And far too early for that. So no eye-contact.

Long enough. They'll have shuffled into their places by now. Just a row of black backs now. And hair. Grey hair, black hair, no hair, hair done for today. But look at that youngster burrowed into his Mum. Must be the wee brother. Just the wrong age. Too old not to know what this is all about, and too young to have to pretend he's brave.

What was that poem he'd done at school, the one with the bit that went '*I will not feel, I will not feel, until I have to?*' Got it right there. Nailed it. At some point there might be a '*have to*', but till then look away and think away, and don't feel. Just the same as the 'don't look down' you told to youngsters on their first climb. 'Keep your eyes on the holds.' MacCaig – that was it. Norman MacCaig. Gone to the fire exit himself now, hadn't he? Don't get many Normans now, do you? Norman Collie though, he was some climber way back then. Skye,

Lakes, the Alps. Tried Nanga Parbat, didn't he? Three dead on that climb. And so it goes on. Christ, enough about deaths.

Off he goes, the minister. Fine. Usually an OK bit. There was a...*professional* quality about ministers that helped you to feel safe. A bit like Mountain Rescue guys. Stick them in a situation of pain and fear and confusion and they know what to do, know what to say, how to keep things calm and ordered. They can even use a bit of humour. Ministers knew that they had a responsibility to keep their own emotions in check, go through the procedures, administer the first aid and get the casualties out of the building safely. Mountain Rescue for the soul. You dealt with the fatality but looked after the survivors too.

It wasn't like when a friend or close relative spoke – which happened more often nowadays. That was more like watching someone solo a route that was maybe a level or two above their normal capabilities. With them you might get the catch in the voice, the sense of someone speaking in that open, unpractised, kind of *naked* way. Speaking words about the deceased that probably wouldn't have been said to him or her even at the end, but now spoken to an audience in a hell of a stressful environment. Now that took guts. Folk had called him brave right from his early climbs as a youngster at Craig-y-Barns, but how was it brave if you weren't frightened? It was different stuff that frightened him. These folk that stood up and talked about their dead mother, or brother or whatever. How could they do that?

Bugger. Another hymn. And one of the favourites too. Always the worst. If you didn't know it there was no problem – you had to concentrate on trying to follow it, just mouthing the words. If you knew it then just the recognition of the first notes sometimes meant you had to check your stance was secure. Just that opening and your hand had to brush below your eye, casual-like.

What was it about a combination of sound waves that could turn on a tiny wee tap in your eye? Even looked the whole thing up in Google, to see what was going on. Fluid, all about fluid. Fluid in your ear and fluid on your eye. The sound of the music was easy: just sound waves travelling through the air and into your ear. Then they went through the ear canal, through some bones and got to the inner ear, where they set some sort of fluid moving. That bent a whole stack of cell-things, like hairs, and the vibrations became the nerve 'watchimacallums' – impulses – that change into what you hear. So you've got this sound – which makes folk, or at least some folk, instantly emotional. Now you're back to the fluids. You've got this fluid protecting your eyes from dust and stuff. But when you get emotional too much fluid is released and the extra stuff comes out as tear drops. Like rain on a climb, water isn't good.

Out on the hill some people get teared up in cold weather, or wind. Didn't happen to him. But here, that was different. Here he had to avoid being stopped by the conspicuous emotion police. 'Excuse me sir, you do realise that you're way over the limit. Just step out of the crematorium please and sit in the car.' It was like your emotion-czar (got to be one of those – surely) had said: 'OK. Enough with this sympathy shit. Sympathy is for wimps. We're going for *empathy* and nothing less.'

Which was why you were now feeling a watery bit of empathy sliding down your cheek as you sang, slowing down as it encountered the friction of stubble. You could feel the slight flattening as it hit the line of your beard, picture the hair glistening damply, like the hairs of a steeped paint brush. Now you had a choice: just let it dry in, hoping there was no more coming, or wipe it away, drawing attention to yourself. And not drawing attention at funerals was a key to a successful conclusion. It was fine of course for the deceased to draw a bit of attention, as he or she wasn't heading for a successful conclusion however you looked at it. So just leave it – it was drying up now. Nothing more following. In control.

A bit of a prayer now, which ironically never caused any problem. You could recognise that the words were *appropriate, dignified, ceremonious*. And therefore no problem, no danger. Standard moves. Like your mate doing the first easy pitch, when you could just let him get on with it, taking in the rope almost absentmindedly. No need to really take the words in, nothing to do with you. Also a good chance to wipe the eyes properly, plus a quick rub at the nose for a bit of camouflage.

A few other bits and pieces but all basically straightforward and easily handled by blanking out some bits, going back in your head to that traverse, picturing the moves. Remembering the concentration that allowed the feeling of control, the enjoyment of danger that most people didn't understand. Then stand up but head down as the family file down and out to form the line to greet the mourners. This was the crux, the nasty overhang you knew was coming, that you had to muscle up and over.

Same approach – work out the moves in advance; put as much protection as possible in place, then commit. Right, let's go. This is where it'd be handy to be blind, or at least carry a white stick. And wear dark glasses. No need for eye contact then. Just stare past, or even walk right past. Let's face it, at a funeral, nobody's going to shout, 'Hey, you wi' the white stick, join the queue like everybody else.' But no, you'd still just draw attention to yourself; folk would make sure you were OK; you'd get taken to the line and some interfering bugger would tell them who you were. And you couldn't pretend to be deaf as well – that'd be pushing it a bit. So you'd still have to say something, and then they'd expect a blind man not to have tears in his eyes wouldn't they? I mean, that's not natural is it, a blind man with tears. Is it? Or is it not? 'The physiological responses of blind men in emotional states'. Put that down as another subject to google.

OK, here we go. *'I will not feel, I will not feel, until I have to.'* Don't look down, look up. Place your hands carefully, keep the breathing steady.

Move on and out. Commit to the move…Enjoy the control. You're the Ice-man. You're the Ice man. Now into the smirr of rain, out of danger. What was the problem? Route completed.

THE CHOOKY

SCENE
Walking paths to the north of Dunkeld.

CAST
(in order of appearance)
MR ROY – *A teacher in charge of a Duke of Edinburgh Award Bronze group (of six boys) from a Perth school.*

GARY; ADAM; JACK; ZACK; HARRY; DEAN

EARLY MORNING

MR ROY: Right folks, you know the drill. Take it in turns to lead, don't stop at checkpoints for more than five minutes, and if you go through gates...?

GARY: Be polite and let the sheep through first.

MR ROY: Very amusing Gary. Now let's get cracking. I'll be following, but no help from me.

ADAM: What if we're in danger, Mr Roy, like frae a coo or sumthin'?

MR ROY: Well Adam, I suggest you just sacrifice Gary while the rest of you make your escape. Now check your direction of travel, estimate your ETA and keep track of the features on your maps. Be away from here in five minutes.

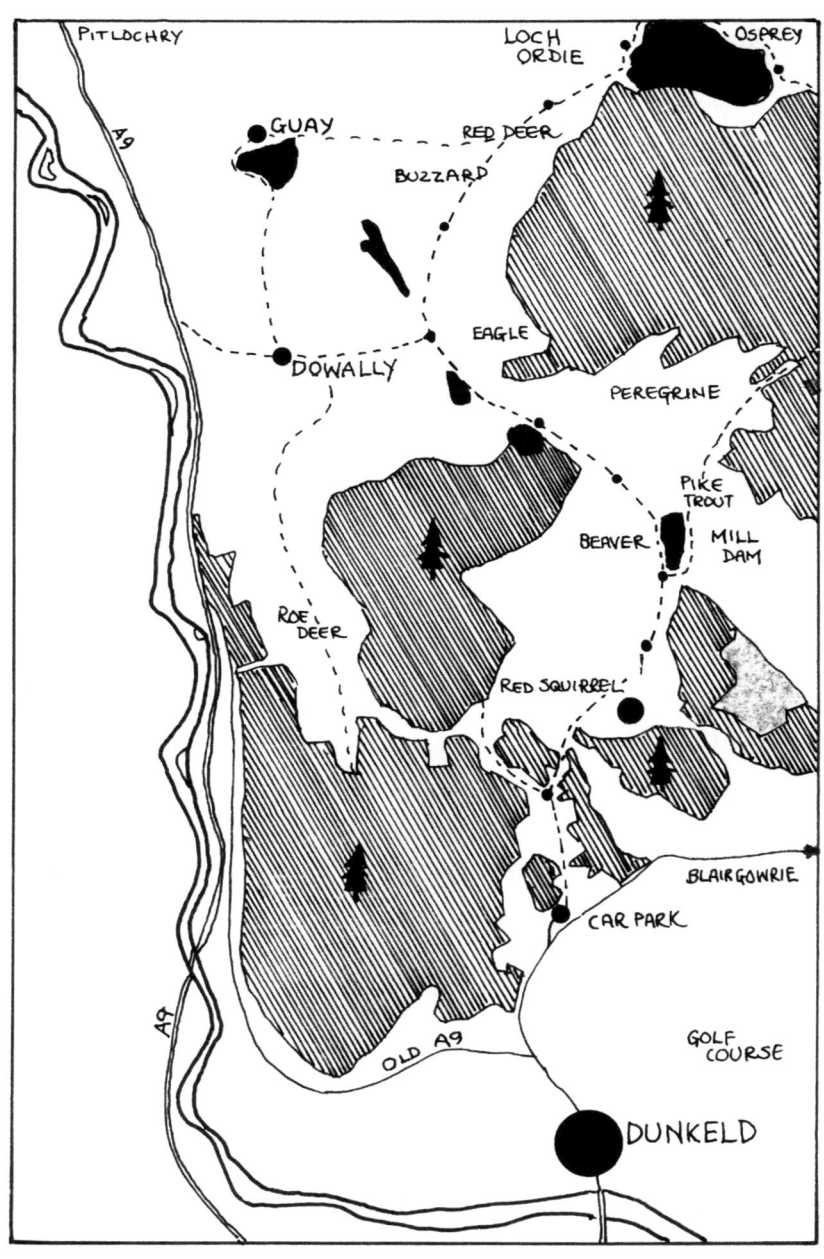

Loch Ordie D of E Walks.

[*The group adopt a version of the Celtic huddle. A compass is laid on top of a map and pushed around like a tumbler on a Ouija board. Every now and then a head pops out and looks around.*]

MR ROY: Maybe I could offer a suggestion. You see that big post you're standing near? Had a look at the top of it?
[*Six heads swivel upwards to see the direction sign, 'Loch Ordie 4 miles'.*]

GARY: Ah saw that sir. Jist wonderin' when these bams would notice.

MR ROY: Yes Gary, of course you did. Now run along children. And no need to scatter breadcrumbs. I'll be following behind.

11:30 – THE FIRST CHECKPOINT

MR ROY: Excellent, you've found the checkpoint. What was the clue? Some element of your pinpoint navigation, or the vast expanse of water in front of you?

JACK: Sir, you do realise that sarcasm is just hostility disguised as humour? It's a passive aggressive manifestation of latent anger. Classic sign of insecurity. Are you insecure sir?

MR ROY: Have you been getting this stuff from Social Education? Or have you been reading your big books again, Jack?

JACK: Actually, sir, it started with *The Simpsons*. It's a popular satirical cartoon. The episode with Professor Frink and his sarcasm detector. I found that interesting and did a little reading into the whole area of sarcasm.

ZACK: He's always reading stuff, Mr Roy. We call him the Professor.

MR ROY: Well Jack, if you're a fan of *The Simpsons* just think of this as *Homer's Odyssey* – so get your crew together and get moving.

12:30 – THE OTHER END OF THE LOCH

MR ROY: Harry, why is that pocket in your rucksack moving?

HARRY: Eh, must be the wind.

MR ROY: Harry, look at the water. It's a flat calm. What's in the pocket?

HARRY: Eh, nothin'.

MR ROY: Well why is 'nothin'' making the pocket of your rucksack move in and out?

HARRY: Must be that 'breathable fabric' sir. There's a wee label that says that. Must be breathin'.

MR ROY: Good try, but doesn't explain the furry snout now sticking out.

DEAN: Sir, it's his hamster, Psycho. Harry wanted him to see a bit of the world. Not much fun you know, in a cage and just goin' round on a wheel all day.

MR ROY: Tell me about it, Dean. I'm a teacher. Anyway, it's a very nice thought Harry, but won't he get cold at night?

HARRY: Naw, he's got a wee sleepin' bag my sister made him out of a sock. Dead cosy. An' he can share our food. Loves Pot Noodle. Fills his cheeks with it an' wee bits hang out.

GARY: Sure that's no' Dean you're thinking about? But Mr Roy, we huv to let wee Psycho come with us, eh? We cannae just send him home. I mean, it would be like that *The Incredible Journey* book we read in English, wi' the dugs an' the cat walkin' hundreds of miles home. Psycho's legs are too wee for that.

JACK: To be fair, the canine and feline protagonists had to walk three hundred miles through the Canadian wilderness, while Dunkeld is six miles away, but Gary has a point, Mr Roy. If there was a RSPCH they'd be down on you like a ton of bricks.

HARRY: Please Mr Roy, look at his wee snout twitchin'. That's fear, that is.

MR ROY: More like the smell inside your rucksack. But OK. Given that the IQ of the group will be raised, Psycho can stay. But if he gets into my tent at any point he's dead meat.

4:30 – THE CAMPSITE

MR ROY: Well done guys, good time. And particularly well done to Psycho for that last hundred metre sprint. I've never seen a hamster on a lead before. You look knackered though, Dean. Thought you were one of the fit ones.

DEAN: It's my rucksack. Weighs a ton.

MR ROY: Let's have a look. [*lifts Dean's rucksack*] Good grief! What have you got in here?

DEAN: Just what was on the list you gave us. Oh, and plenty water.

MR ROY: Well you're all carrying water. How much have you got? More than a litre?

DEAN: Eh, I think it's five litres. My Mum said to take it. She said there might be dead sheep in the burns.

MR ROY: Five litres! That must weigh…?

JACK: Five kilograms.

MR ROY: Thank you Jack. Now Dean, I've been doing this for around fifteen years and I've never seen a dead sheep in any burn. I think you should pour out the water and I promise you, if we *do* come across a sheep in any of the burns I will personally donate all my water to you. Now find level spots for your tents and get them up. Could be rain soon.

[*The boys start to erect their tents while Mr Roy gives friendly advice.*]

MR ROY: No Adam, the fly-sheet won't fit inside the tent. It's still bigger than the inner even if you stand far away. Zack, I'd like those guy ropes in line with the seams. Yes, I know you're not good at geometry. There aren't enough tent pegs, Dean? Have a look under your groundsheet. Yes, I'm aware that it's pegged down. You'll have to unpeg it, find the rest of the pegs, and start again.

[*Eventually the two tents are up, to Mr Roy's satisfaction, or close enough.*]

MR ROY: Now, a very important matter. Toilet arrangements. You can pee where you like so long as it's fifty metres from the tents and the same distance from the burn. But if you need to do more than pee then you need to use this. [*He holds out a supermarket size plastic bag.*] And then take it back with you.

DEAN: What! All of us? In there?

ADAM: Then somebody's got to *carry it?*

GARY: You're jokin'. Six of us usin' that?

MR ROY: No joke boys. [*He puts his hand into the bag and brings out a trowel.*] You dig a hole with this, do your business, then trowel it over. What did you think I meant? [*chuckling*]

DEAN: Had us goin' there sir. My imagination was runnin' riot. An' no' in a good way.

ADAM: That was cruel. That's goin' down in our expedition log.

MR ROY: Always my favourite moment of any expedition. Now, get your meals on, and when you wash up make sure you do what?

GARY: Check for piranhas?

MR ROY: Not quite what I was thinking, Gary. Make sure it's downstream from where you take your drinking water. And Dean, see that hill up there? That's where this burn starts. Why don't you take a hike up there, just in case I'm wrong about the sheep.

[*The boys cook their meals, wash up, then disappear into their tents, out of the rain. Around 11.00 p.m. the chatter finally ceases and a perfect silence descends. A silence punctuated by an angry yell.*]

MR ROY: Harry! Get this flaming hamster out of my tent!

NEXT MORNING

MR ROY: Come on, come on! Up you get, get your breakfasts cooked and then pack up. Absolutely nothing left to show we've been here. Leaving in forty minutes.

[*The boys slowly emerge from the tents, cook breakfasts, and begin to pack up the tents. Then the inspection of the campsite begins.*]

MR ROY: Who had pasta last night?

ADAM: Me and Zack.

MR ROY: So what I'm looking at here are not particularly large maggots you brought along to use for fishing bait but rather the remains of your dinner from last night?

GARY: What do y'think? Seven?

DEAN: Nah, just six.

JACK: I agree, just six. Not personal enough for seven.

MR ROY: What on earth are you talking about?

JACK: It's your sarcasm rating system. We've decided to

grade your sarcastic remarks. We take into account originality, humorous content and personal vindictiveness. Don't worry though, we'd be quite interested to experience a perfect ten.

MR ROY: In that case…Adam, Zack, be good lads and pick that pasta up. Thanks a lot.

GARY: [to Jack] That's confusin'. Was he bein' nice or not?

JACK: I'd say it's the classic 'lull into a false sense of security' ploy. Gets us relaxed before hitting us with a nine or ten.

MR ROY: Well, anything that keeps you alert and on your toes. And the added bonus for me is that I now know you'll get annoyed by my pleasant disposition. In the meantime, gentlemen, work out you ETA for the next checkpoint and any points of reference you expect to see on the way. I'm staying here for a while then I'll catch you up.

GARY: That was still sort of pleasant, wasn't it? Or did I miss somethin' sneaky?

JACK: No, but keep your ears open. I'm not sure how long Mr Roy can keep this up.

ADAM: That's the pasta picked up. Psycho helped with the wee bits. Cheeks are pure bulgin'. Let's look at the map.

LATER THAT MORNING

DEAN: Are you sure this is it? [showing the rest his map] If you check the grid references should we not be there? [He runs his finger up the side of the map, then along.]

ADAM: That would be the middle of Blairgowrie, tube.

HARRY: Yeah, you went up the map then along. Mind what we were told – along the street then up the stairs. And that puts us…there. Right at the junction of the track and the path. Bear Grylls eat your heart out…Maybe he *would* eat your heart out, you know, like, to survive.

ADAM: Yeah, this is it, and ten minutes ahead of schedule. Time for a lie down.

HARRY: Hey, Mr Roy'll be impressed. Think he's far behind us?

MR ROY: [*stepping out from behind nearby trees*] Not too far behind, Harry. But good going. Took me a while to work past you and wait here.

GARRY: Was that…?

JACK: No, I think it was just a straightforward compliment and a statement of fact. Sarcasm still seems to be missing. Quite impressive.

MR ROY: Thank you, Jack. Now, who led that leg?

ADAM: Me an' Harry. And we saw all the features on the way. The burn coming down on our left, the crags on the right, then the bridge.

MR ROY: Good stuff. And what about you, Dean? Rucksack lighter today?

DEAN: Yeah, it's great. An' I'm no' hearin that sloshin' noise in my ears.

MR ROY: Excellent, though I'm not convinced the sloshing noise was water. Now who's leading the next section?

[*Halfway along the next stage, Jack is walking beside Mr Roy at the back of the group.*]

JACK: Isn't it strange? We're all roughly the same age, but look at the differences in height.

MR ROY: I presume you know why that is?

JACK: Genetics, nutrition, puberty, I'd suggest.

MR ROY: So we've got Gary looking a bit like an Ent from *The Lord of the Rings*, all big, slow strides. Then Harry, more like a hobbit, hidden behind that huge rucksack.

JACK: Interesting literary reference but Harry reminds me more of Kafka.

MR ROY: Kafka? You've read Kafka?

JACK: Well, not everything. But I recently read *Metamorphosis.* You know how Gregor Samsa turns into a beetle? That's what Harry reminds me of, scuttling along with his legs and arms sticking out from that black rucksack, with its shiny rain cover.

MR ROY: Eh…yes…quite an imagination you've got there, Jack. Do a lot of fiction reading as well as your psychological research?

JACK: As much as I can. But I'm pretty busy at the moment. Duke of Edinburgh, orchestra, rugby, science club, homework.

MR ROY: So you don't think teenagers are all lazy then?

JACK: Some are, I suppose. But look at us. We're all doing loads of extra stuff, as well as school work.

GARY: [*turning round*] Hey, sir. What's that big bird up there? Is it an eagle?

MR ROY: Ah, well spotted, Gary. Not an eagle though. Anyone know? Shut up Jack.

HARRY: Is it an osprey?

DEAN: Yeah, must be. You're supposed to see them round here if you're lucky. Better mind Psycho, Harry. He'd make a nice wee snack. One gulp.

ADAM: Do they not just eat fish, Mr Roy?

MR ROY: Ninety-nine percent of the time. But they have been seen eating rodents. Anyway, put that in your logbooks later. What's that you've seen so far?

ADAM: Some deer, the what d'you call them at the burn... dippers, that osprey. And a hamster.

GARY: Look, that's our checkpoint up there. The bridge. We're motorin' now guys, eh?

DEAN: I'm getting used to this rucksack, too. Doesn't seem as heavy.

GARY: That's because you've ate about ten pounds of food. Guys, want to just walk on? Only what, 4K to the finish.

DEAN: Yeah, let's go. Back to civilisation. What have you missed?

ADAM: Chips. I could murder a plate of chips.

HARRY: My bed. My pillow. My duvet.

ZACK: My mobile. Must be dozens of texts from girls

wonderin' where I am. An' maybe one from the Chooky Embra askin' how I'm getting on.

JACK: What about you, Mr Roy? What do you want to get back to?

MR ROY: Silence. I'd like to just sit for a while – in silence. A long while. Right, you said you want to get to the finish, so last bit of navigation check then let's crack on.

JACK: [*holding map*] So it's… four and a bit kilometres. That's… one hour?

GARRY: And look there. About 2K an' then there's the two hills on the right, with the saddle thing in between.

ZACK: Then the hill with crags on the left.

HARRY: Then the track hits the road and the van'll be there and we get our boots off.

GARRY: Are we the best navigators you've seen, sir?

MR ROY: Well, put it this way. If I were in Room 36, and wanted guides to take me next door to Room 37, then you lot would definitely scrape in to my top ten possibilities.

THE BOYS: [*all together*] Ten!

The Superiority of Mankind

Feeling good, must be fit
Burned off those guys at last
From behind we hear a bark
A golden streak flies past

Looking back, hill half done
Slowly gaining height
Deer catch scent, antlers rise
Thunder out of sight

Snowfield climbed, cutting steps
Sweating in the chill
Mountain hare, flash of white
Romps across the hill

Summit reached, sense of pride
Crack that can of beer
Look up now, ravens circling
That a laugh we hear?

The Walkers

At first it was just a few thousand, spread across the country. Not till that number grew to tens of thousands did the story make the news, as one of those 'and now' items found at the end of the bulletins, between the sport and the weather.

'Walking fever seems to be hitting Britain. For weeks now pubs and clubs have been emptier, TV viewing figures down, buses less crowded. But pavements and parks, highways and byways, are busy with pedestrians of every age. In London many workers are deserting the Underground in favour of a healthy walk to work. Is this just a passing phase or are we seeing a change in our habits?'

However, the story gradually rose towards the headlines as the tens of thousands became hundreds of thousands.

'The urge to walk for hours at a time seems to be intensifying significantly. This is not just normal countryside rambling. People have taken to walking alone or in groups, along town and city roads, round parks, through housing and industrial estates. They don't seem to want to get anywhere, they just want to walk. Groups of men and women have even been seen roaming through the night along otherwise deserted streets. They pose no apparent danger, content to walk along silently or in conversation with others. Medical opinion is that the phenomenon is a kind of psychosomatic event which is expected to end as quickly as it started.'

But rather than slowing down matters accelerated, as more and more of the population were on the move: all classes, all ages, some striding, some strolling, some only able to shuffle. The weather made no difference – outdoor clothing sales rose and umbrellas went up. It became obvious that many were walking rather than driving to their places of work, were walking longer and longer distances, were walking in areas normally people-free. The story could now be filed under 'scare'.

'Politicians are becoming increasingly alarmed at what is now being seen as the national threat posed by 'the walkers'. Latest figures estimate that the number of people marching around the country has been rising daily and currently measures around three million. Some are unemployed, some are retired, but employers are reporting many instances of individuals walking out of their places of work. We talked to Professor Nicholas Groves, of King's College London, a leading expert on 'mass hysterical conditions', as these events might be described by academics.'

'Professor Groves, how unusual a phenomenon is this?'

'Unusual but certainly not unique. There are well-documented cases throughout history and indeed throughout the world. As far back as 1518 Strasbourg saw what was known as 'The Dancing Plague', when people danced for days without rest, some even dying. Nearer our own time was the 'Tanganyika Laughter Epidemic' of 1962. Ninety-five schoolgirls were affected, some for over a fortnight, and the epidemic spread to other schools. In 2007, in Mexico City, there was an incident almost the reverse of the one we are discussing. An outbreak of mass hysteria amongst hundreds of adolescent females resulted in them having *difficulty* in walking. And only a few years ago, in 2018, we had the fainting pandemic across mainland Europe. But the different factors regarding this walking outbreak are the number of people involved and the degree of control shown by the participants. Those points, particularly the latter, make me hesitate to label this as a 'normal' hysterical event, if you forgive the oxymoron.'

'And should we be worried? Do these walkers pose any danger to the general public?'

'As things stand, no danger at all. These are not antisocial groups in any sense. They do no damage to the environment, they interact in a friendly fashion. They seem content to talk to each other and look about them as they walk.'

'And what about danger to themselves and their health?'

'Quite the reverse, so far. Many have agreed to be examined both physically and psychologically and the overwhelming evidence is positive. The exercise is extremely beneficial to most. They lose weight and those tested show markedly decreased stress levels. Of course there have been blisters, the odd fall, a number of heart problems, but that is hardly surprising given the numbers. Taking the demographic as a whole they are notably healthier than the average.'

'But couldn't the walking become obsessive?'

'Well of course that would be problematic, but, as I explained, this activity could be classed as a controlled behaviour. Apart from devoting several hours a day to their perambulations most of those involved are leading otherwise normal, indeed unusually healthy lives.'

The news media were disappointed at this refusal to suggest drama or danger. They preferred 'hysteria' to 'controlled behaviour', often translating it into the more tabloid-friendly 'madness' or 'craziness', with the walkers variously described as 'loony', 'loopy' or the helpfully alliterative 'wacky'. Reporters were sent out looking for manifestations of such 'wackiness'. They walked alongside their targets – the slower moving or the possibly eccentric – firing their stock questions, similar to the ones asked of celebrities in the London Marathon.

'How do you feel?'

'Fine. Nice to be out in the fresh air.'

'Is it not tiring?'

'Yeah. But in a good way, y'know.'

'What made you start this walking?'

'Dunno. Just felt I wanted to.'

'What do you think about when you're walking?'

'Just, like, life 'n stuff. Puts things a bit clearer. And you can talk to other people. You know, really talk.'

Editors, already worried about their catastrophically falling circulation figures, harangued the returning reporters and sent them out again to get some 'real' stories.

'Phone the hospitals. Get some heart attacks. Use your police contacts for Christ's sake. These are mobs on the streets – where's the violence?'

But the material they came back with was thin stuff. There was the occasional bit of minor road rage as motorists found streets temporarily 'pedestrianised'. People in normally quiet estates phoned police about 'gangs' invading their Neighbourhood Watched environments, but the 'gangs' turned out to be pleasant, polite and happy to admire the gardens they passed. The only items which went missing were a number of reporters, who became walkers themselves.

Numbers grew and reports increased of changes in the lifestyles of the population. More and more cars sat idle; those which were driven often had to slow down where roads filled with groups of walkers; more wheelchairs were seen on pavements and roads; overtime was refused; many commuters found jobs locally, despite lower salaries. By and large, most people were still combining their daily walking with the 'normal' activities of working and shopping but they walked early in the morning, at lunch breaks, after work. The large number of retired or unemployed walked whenever they wished and, increasingly, wherever.

The Government of the day was concerned, as all governments are when the population surprises them. An emergency committee met in Cabinet Office Briefing Room A, where the Prime Minister went round her key Departments in turn.

"Home Secretary. Your issues?"

Downing Street was concerned.

"People. People behaving...uncharacteristically. No actual trouble as such but some Chief Constables are concerned at the sheer number of people on the streets, in parks, woods, etcetera. In lots of places the numbers would normally constitute illegal assemblies – but nobody has actually organised them and there are just too many of them for any useful action to be taken. Oh, and many rank and file officers are putting in requests to leave their cars and walk beats again."

"George, transport must be affected. Yes?"

"Mainly positively. Some problems when streets are taken

over temporarily by groups of pedestrians, but that's balanced by the huge reduction in car use. Nobody seems interested in the arterial roads so that's no problem. Bus companies have already compressed timetables due to reduced demand and are looking for increased subsidies. But traffic accidents, well they're down considerably."

"Positive news from Health, I believe. Tell us more, Helen."

"As we already knew, walking is, in general terms, good for us. My experts tell me more specifically that it improves triglyceride levels so lowers blood pressure. It increases concentrations of norepinephrine, which moderates responses to stress. As a low-level activity people can also direct their executive functioning to internal matters – in other words think more. On the negative side a few heart attacks have been caused by older people overdoing it, and there is an increased incidence of minor muscle strain, but overall the effects are nothing short of dramatic."

"Sounds excellent – apart from the 'think more'. Not sure about that. No Helen, just a joke. But you're not so happy, David?"

"Putting it mildly, Katherine. Economically it's a bloody disaster. We're looking at more and more people, from every area of the economy, switching off from their primary function – keeping the economy moving."

"But they are, in general, still working, yes?"

"In general, yes. Have to bloody eat don't they? But we're seeing a staggering drop in overtime from those who don't really require the money. And more and more early retirements, some from very senior positions – even in the City, for God's sake. Financial traders are starting to cut down their hours because they 'fancy going out for a walk'! At least the low-paid can't afford that luxury. But they just walk in the bloody evening instead of sitting at home. It's unnatural. And I've got the Autumn Statement to present in two weeks."

The PM paused for a moment, then looked round the table, brow furrowing as she noticed the empty chair.

"Where's Ken?"

A few pairs of eyes looked round the room as if suspecting that the Deputy PM was for some reason hiding somewhere. Other participants suddenly found their notes fascinating. Then the Chancellor cleared his throat and addressed the PM.

"Thought you knew. Apparently he's gone for a walk."

The PM rolled her eyes, always a warning sign that her famous equanimity was being tested to the point where she felt the need to release a bit of cathartic temper.

"So, ladies and gentlemen,' she said, her voice dangerously soft, 'you've outlined the problems wonderfully well. Now who can give me some *fucking* solutions?"

After a short but tense silence Peter Fraser, Minister without Portfolio, raised a hand a few inches off the polished table.

"It's the internet, Prime Minister. The social media thingy. I spoke to my two kids about this and they laughed and told me it was just another meme going viral."

"Meme? What the hell's a meme?"

"Comes from the Greek, Prime Minister. 'Mimema', meaning 'imitated thing'. You know, like 'mime'. Richard Dawkins turned it into 'meme'. Richard Dawkins, he's a…"

"Yes, Peter, I know who Richard Dawkins is. We were at Oxford together. So where exactly does this meme fit into the subject at hand?"

"Well, it's just shorthand for some idea that spreads from person to person. Of course I told them that even I knew this walking thing was all over the internet, but so were lots of things and that's where they remained, on the internet till the next big thing came along. Social media doesn't usually make people do things, I said, just talk about them. Well, apart from funny dances and pouring iced water over people. But it did get me thinking, so I called in someone I was told about. Dr Adam Gordon, an expert in 'Collective Obsessional Behaviour'. Cutting out the jargon, he reckons it's a perfect storm. You've got the original psychosomatic event; the internet allows it to spread further and faster than is usually the case; and the positive effects – endorphins etc – encourage repetition."

"And this expert of yours,' asked the Prime Minister, 'has he anything to say about how long this 'perfect storm' might last?"

"Not really. This is a new phenomenon. But of the three factors above, the one that can be worked on by us is the internet effect. He reckons that might be what has caused this to spread so widely and last so long."

"Right, Home Secretary. Your area I think. Can we sort this?"

"Shouldn't be a problem, now that we're out of the European Court of Human Rights. But perhaps better if none of you know exactly what my people might do. Just leave it with me."

A few weeks later there was already a significant drop off in the number of walkers. The 'management' of internet traffic was both subtle and gradual, making no waves except amongst those dedicated to the uncovering of state interference. They were fed some factually incorrect material by apparent whistle-blowers and thus discredited. The mainstream media had no interest in them anyway, preferring to concentrate on 'Britain Returning to Sanity'. In another part of the strategy selected medical experts were frequently interviewed on news programmes, armed with statistics suggesting there were many hidden health risks in over-walking. In a neat piece of spin the now rising incidence of heart and blood pressure problems was ascribed to the walking outbreak itself rather than the decline in exercise. Within months the Government could point to rapidly improving economic output. The numbers of regular walkers were still high, but now at a level which could be described by social observers as an interesting cultural trend rather than a threat.

On a sunny February morning the Prime Minister and her Director of Communications and Strategy looked through the newspapers together. In the main they were satisfyingly neutral while some were pleasingly positive about the economic indicators. A few – the usual suspects – criticised the negative trends in physical and mental health.

"Not bad for midterm," she purred. "Any ideas about the health issues?"

"I've been thinking about that. Maybe time for a bit of fresh blood. Show you're not complacent. And he's not exactly popular, is he?"

"My thinking too." Her forefinger paused briefly before engaging the intercom. "Amanda, fix an appointment with the Secretary of State for Health, please. This afternoon."

Drawing to a Halt

It started with a virgin landscape,
Featureless to the far borders.
From that whiteout the climber appeared,
Head, torso, then limbs.
You knew he was a climber,
A winter mountaineer.
Bobble hat and crampons,
On his back a massive rucksack
With frying pan dangling,
On his chin black bristles
Like Desperate Dan's.

Now arose steep, jagged peaks
Like a hospital patient's chart
Or the Footsie in frantic flux.
Identikit Christmas trees,
Four ski jump branches each side,
Grew swiftly in random clumps.
Above were those fluffy Simpson clouds
And stiff winged birds
Hovering motionless,
Just black V's in the sky.

Paisley pattern sweat appeared,
Dripping past a lolling tongue
Like a panting Labrador's,
And tiny smoke-ring circles
Rose from a Munch-scream mouth
To meet a larger cloud-shape
Encircling a capitalised word
And many, many exclamation marks.

Above, a gigantic snowball careered down
Motionlessly, shedding filaments of black.
One time slip and two dimensions later
It sprouted arms, legs, a bobbled head,
Before a pause, as time stood still
And Fate hovered above, and animation
Was suspended...

Till black lightning struck
With fatal force,
Obliterating the tragic-comic scene
With graphite gouges.
The landscape was pulverised
Into a chaotic asterisk,
Expanding as it flew
Towards a black hole of
oblivion,
In the corner of the room.

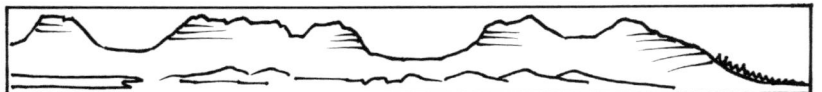

Tri Uairean's a'Bhladhna

There are different types of climbing/walking clubs. There are ones such as the legendary Creag Dhu, known for hard men, hard climbing, and the occasional pub brawl. The one I have been a member of for nearly thirty years is unlike the Creag Dhu, except in the minds of its members. It meets for three weekends every year, with various sub-groups meeting for hill walks in between. The members are from the Perth or Dundee areas, apart from one who comes back to Scotland from that mecca for Munroists – Surrey. We are officially known as *Tri Uairean's A'Bhladhna Mountaineering Club,* which is a fine name, redolent of misty isles and glens. It marks the club out as being at one with our country's culture and linguistic background. However, since non-Gaelic speakers find it quite difficult to say and impossible to spell, it is rarely used. For all we know the Gaelic might even be a bit dodgy. Members prefer the more down to earth, means what it says on the tin version – *The Three Times a Year Club.* Significantly, the 'club' part is usually dropped, since we are unsure if we fit that definition. It is a proud boast that there are absolutely no rules, headquarters, entry qualifications or unusual handshakes. It is a 'club' only in the sense that members seem to turn up regularly at given locations, three times a year, and climb as many or as few mountains as they wish. This flexibility means that, apart from the dozen regulars, other people might turn up. It's assumed that they must be the friends of someone, but for all we know they may simply have seen an open door and a lot of beer.

Now we don't boast about this but between us we have completed more than 320 ascents of Everest. I know, quite impressive. To be more accurate we have climbed the *equivalent* of those ascents. On our twenty year anniversary we worked out that with an average of 203 Munros per person, and with Munros averaging 1,000 metres, this gave a height of 2,846,000 metres. Everest is 8,848 metres, giving us that impressive 320 ascents. Of course, we have been adding Munros for nearly eight more years, so there should by now be many more Everests. But given the slowdown in hills achieved – what some might call a failure of collective will – the number might only have risen marginally. Anyway, why climb to the top of Everest? After that it would be all downhill. As a group of committed supporters of feminism we would echo the words of Junko Tabei, the first woman to climb Everest: '*I can't understand why men make all this fuss about Everest – it's only a mountain.*'

Instead of expensive, thrill-seeking expeditions to the Alps or the Himalayas the *Three Times* have made their excitement in the Scottish hills. Let's start with one weekend in Torridon. (This is where my decision to omit names from this account makes sense.) To be honest, drink had been taken when three middle aged scamps decided on a rum-fuelled night-time ascent of Liathach. After reaching a respectable height sanity returned, as did they.

This was their best decision of the night, as involvement of Mountain Rescue would have been embarrassing.

'What navigation equipment do you have, sir?'

'Eh, two half-cut geography teachers.'

'And what about emergency rations?'

'No problem – we've still got two bottles of rum.'

Another incident occurred when we were being more sensible and practising ice axe braking in the Mamores. One participant built up too much speed and soon resembled a winter sports skeleton racer, without the skeleton. Half of the group tried to arrest his plummet towards a drop while the other half threw themselves on the bits of equipment which sprang off like debris from a human avalanche. Flask, sandwiches, ice axe, sangfroid, sense of direction – one by one they splintered off. It was exactly like a Saturn rocket shedding its booster rockets – except for the direction of travel. He eventually ground to a halt inches (as we remember it) from a terrifying precipice (as we remember it) and shamefaced companions had to return the bits of gear they were stowing in their rucksacks.

But perhaps the most dangerous incident the *Three Times* was ever involved in occurred in the shadow of the Inaccessible Pinnacle on the Cuillin Ridge, Skye. We had climbed the easier east ridge and abseiled down. Now we were watching a young female climber solo the challenging west side. Clearly upset by this assault on an obviously phallic symbol one of our group momentarily forgot his normal respect for female achievement, shouting out, "Not bad for a girlie!" Not since Tam o'Shanter cried out '*Weel done, Cutty-sark!*' has there been a more dangerous and provocative (and patronising) exclamation, followed by the hastiest of retreats. It's not easy to run along the Cuillin Ridge, but we did.

"Not bad for a girlie!"

Despite what is said by wives and significant others a lot of hill walking does still go on. Although leaving the pub might seem risky behaviour no one has ever been *really* lost on a *Three Times* weekend, though members have put up some very innovative ascent routes. Records show that on more than one occasion peaks were successfully ascended but, on closer inspection of maps, it was found that they were not necessarily the peaks aimed for. Technology has come to the rescue in recent years. With the advent of GPS navigation systems we are now able to say with absolute precision which wrong top we are standing on.

Strangely enough religion has played a part in the slower rate of Munro-bagging. In the early days we walked on both Saturday and Sunday. Some hardy members still do so, but most of the club have become increasingly religious and keep the Sabbath as a day of rest. Very occasionally religion takes over completely and members begin the weekend keeping the Jewish Sabbath then switch to Christianity on Sunday. This ecumenical approach, however, is never allowed to affect the traditional Saturday night worship of the 'Holy Spirits' known as single malts.

Yes, it cannot be denied that members occasionally take a drink. '*They speak of my drinking but never think of my thirst*' is an old Scottish proverb. Strangely enough it is also one of the slogans of the *Three Times*. We have found that the two chief requirements for a meet venue are proximity to good mountains and even closer proximity to a good pub. This is why, in a club survey of favourite venues, the winner was close to the Cuillins, next door to a pub, and a hundred metres from a distillery. Synchronicity at work. There are, of course, dangers associated with strong drink. As many readers will know, it can cause thirst in the night. This happened to one of our number, who luckily found a glass of water next to where he was sleeping. Less luckily he swallowed both the water and the contact lenses floating therein. Some people have eyes in the back of their heads. One of us can claim to have had them in a more interesting place.

Anyone who frequents the pubs used by climbers and walkers knows that they often feature live folk music. Sometimes it is played by musicians paid by the hostelry; sometimes, with the permission of the publican, it is created by the *Three Times*. Yes, our unique selling point is not putting up first ascents but the ability to fill a pub with music. For a club of our size an astonishing number of people can play instruments, ranging through fiddle, guitar and piano to the more basic pots and pans percussion...and a few people who are just about able to bang on tables in an approximate rhythm. The two leading members of the ensemble actually get paid to play in various venues, and when playing and singing on club weekends the entire ensemble has been given free drink, invitations to return, caused lock-ins, and were gifted a bottle of whisky by a landlord in Portnalong, Skye. This has been kept, unopened, as our only piece of club memorabilia. We are hoping that one day it might take its place in a Scottish Mountaineering Museum alongside early home-made ice axes, or Tom Weir's bunnet. Music, however, does not always result in harmony. Occasionally other musicians join in, and this caused 'The Great Schism of Glen Clova'. The proper musicians began to play what the rest of us regarded as 'diddly-dee' stuff. So we retired to a back room with the intention of singing the songs we enjoyed – the cheery ones about dead soldiers, starving widows and industrial pollution in a '*Dirty Old Town*'. Unfortunately no one could remember many of the words, so we just played pool.

So there we are, a set of ingredients recognisable to anyone who has walked in the hills with good companions. They could be a reflection of Scottish culture: music, drink, humour, companionship – and all in the setting of a romantic landscape.

Alternatively it's just the history of a bunch of guys who meet up every now and then, go for a walk, then have a few pints and a song. And what could be better than that?

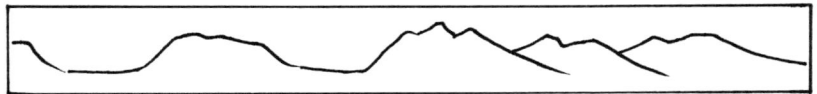

THE LAST MUNRO

THE MINIBUS LURCHED untidily into the makeshift layby and disgorged its passengers. Limbs were stretched, boots laced up, rucksacks swung on. All this to a background of cheerfully insulting banter.

"You got a sleepin' bag under that jacket, Alex?"

"Hey Cameron, remember to pack your sense of direction this time?"

"Least I don't have left an' right printed on my boots."

A hand banged a metallic tattoo on the side of the vehicle, producing a few shouts, then silence. Les Stewart addressed the group.

"Ladies and gentlemen – and you, Alex – this is a solemn moment. We are about to embark upon the ascent of Gregor McKay's final Munro. It's only taken him thirty years, the lazy bugger."

"Hey! Mind the language in front o' young Sarah here."

"Sorry Cameron. Sarah, dear, I apologise. Bet you never hear any bad words at school, eh? Or from your Grandad Cameron. Anyhow, for those of you who're not regular walkers don't worry. Gregor clearly thought about this thirty years ago and he's left himself a nice easy one for last. There's a good path up till near the top then a bit of a plateau an' a grand big cairn to prove we're where we thought we were."

"Not always been the case, eh Les?"

"Don't worry Alex, once we're back in the pub stories will be told. Anyway, Jesus was only forty days in the wilderness.

Gregor had hoped that more of a fuss would have been made of his last Munro.

Some of us old ones have been wandering in it for forty years. Bound to have got lost a couple of times. Right, enough talk, everybody ready? Let's get this show on the road. Lead on McKay! And damned be him who first cries 'Hold! Enough!'"

"You been lookin' up your book of quotations again?"

"Just comes from having an educated mind, Cameron."

"Play on."

"What's that, Sarah?"

"Play on," repeated Sarah. "It's '*Play on Macduff*', not '*Lead on*'. Everybody misquotes that."

"Oh very good, lass. Thanks for puttin' me right," said Les, thinking *smart arse*.

The group walked on, breaking into twos and threes on the initial broad path. The mood was cheerful – it wasn't every day that someone completed their round of Munros, all 283 of them. So there was a general feeling that something significant was about to be marked, a feeling which was not, however, shared entirely by the soon-to-be Munroist himself. Gregor McKay had a tidy mind. He didn't like tasks not completed properly. And there was a nagging suspicion in his mind that the completion of the task in hand was possibly, perhaps, just maybe – questionable.

It had started about a week ago. He'd sat one evening, a small whisky in his hand, his dog-eared Munro book in his lap. In this book, the *Bible* of every Munro bagger, each Munro is listed and a route described, along with a simple map. Each three thousand foot peak Gregor had climbed was marked with a tick, along with the date and sometimes the name or names of any companions. As he turned the pages he remembered memorable days of brilliant weather giving panoramic views from the tops, and more typical Scottish days navigating through mist and seeing nothing but a wispy grey blanket. Any memory of scores of other peaks had faded – all he knew was that they had been 'knocked off', since they had been ticked off.

Then he got to page 201, and remembered what he had either forgotten or perhaps unconsciously pushed into a shadowy corner of his mind. Beinn a' Chlaidheimh – the 'hill of the sword'. There was the tick, one of the 283 symbols of success, confirmations of completion. But right alongside the tick was another mark, a denotation of doubt, a question mark. Even more questionable, it had been pencilled in, rubbed out, but was still visible as a grey indentation in the white paper.

The date reminded him that it had been twenty years since he and Dave Sinclair had started that climb. It had been a winter ascent in deep snow that got deeper as the day wore on, the kind of thing he'd been up for at that age. The conditions were close to whiteout, reducing both visibility and contrast and causing distorted orientation. They were competent enough – perhaps foolhardy enough – to reach the narrow ridge leading up to the summit, and they found a reasonable sized cairn. Whether it was indeed at the highest point could not be judged by eyesight, but they felt rather than saw that the ground ahead dipped down rather than up. They knew the peak had no summit-confirming triangulation pillar so a cairn would mark the top, and they, well Dave, quickly took the decision that this was the correct cairn.

After a long and difficult descent they went back to the hostel to change into dry gear. Over a mug of coffee Gregor got out his Munro book and prepared to pencil off another completion.

"You absolutely sure that was the top?" he had asked.

"You kidding? Course it was. We can navigate, can't we?" Dave was never anything less than confident, though his confidence with navigation, driving and chatting up women was not necessarily matched by his abilities.

"Might put a question mark," Gregor had said, pencilling one in.

"Fuck off, get it ticked. Cairn, ground going down, superb navigation – what's the problem?"

Maybe Dave was right, Gregor had thought. He always worried too much. He had confidence in his own navigation. And it had been a long drive to get there. He turned his pencil round, like a compass needle swinging from north to south, used its eraser, then marked the page with a tick.

But now, two decades on, Gregor was walking between

Sarah and Cameron, feeling like that princess in the Hans Christian Anderson tale, the one who could feel the pea irritating her through twenty mattresses and twenty eiderdowns. Except his pea was a three thousand foot lump buried under another 282 similar lumps.

"Mr McKay..."

"Call me Gregor. Fifteen year olds get that privilege."

"Gregor, how do people know that you've climbed all those mountains? Couldn't you just say that you've done them? I mean, does anyone check?"

"No, there's no check. No Munro police."

"It's up to you to be honest," said Cameron. "Anyway, what would be the point? You'd just be cheatin' yourself, wouldn't you?"

"But why do you want to do these ones anyway? I mean, are they the best mountains?"

"Most of them are good climbs, Sarah," replied Gregor. "Though some are pretty boring. And there's a lot that don't make Munro height that are great hills. They're called..."

"...Corbetts, I know. And Donalds and Grahams. So why bother doing the boring ones just because they're on a list? That's like...it's like reading all the books in a library that are over a certain number of pages, even though you aren't enjoying them and there's better ones that are shorter."

"Jeez, Sarah," winced Cameron. "Don't hold back, love. Cheer the man up. Always been a bit o' a nippy sweetie this one. Fifteen goin' on forty."

"It's fine. Good to think about it. I mean she's right in a way. It *is* just a list."

"And I bet lots of people have cheated with one or two," added Sarah. "At least the men might. Mum says all men cheat."

"Aye, she does," sighed Cameron. "Over and over again. We've heard her. But this is Gregor we're talking about, not that useless father of yours. Gregor's got integrity. Now let's change the subject. We're in God's playground here and it's a happy day we're meant to be havin', eh Gregor?"

Gregor managed a smile and a "Sure, Cameron" but the smile was fleeting. He increased his pace to walk on his own for a while, using the narrowing path as an excuse. He tried to empty his mind and just take in the surroundings: the path winding up towards and through a rocky band; the horizon he knew would be a false summit; the loch below already apparently shrunken in size from loch to lochan. But try as he might four syllables beat a simple rhythm in his head: 'Beinn a' Claidheimh, Beinn a' Claidheimh. Beinn a' Claidheimh.'

After a few minutes he was caught up by an out of breath Les.

"Hey pal, what's the rush? You want to make this last – an you're goin' too fast for some of the less fit ones back there."

Gregor dropped his pace and Les carried on chatting, his default mode.

"Funny thing about Munros, isn't it? Lots of folk, like me, get to about forty left, think they'll finish them, never do. End up doin' the same ones again because they're closer. An' then, I know a few folk that won't touch the summit cairns or the trig points – don't want to be baggin' them at all. Another guy I know's done them all except one. Won't climb it – says it's like these carpet makers that always put one deliberate mistake in the pattern. Persians, Navajo do that. Amish too, I think. Different reasons but all a bit spiritual – stuff about perfection only belongin' to their God."

"What you trying to tell me, Les? Is this Zen and the art of Munro bashin'? Saying I shouldn't climb this?" Gregor laughed, but uncertainly.

"Naw, not you. You're too borin' for that stuff. Always thought you'd finish them. You were always counting them down, planning the next one to go for. Mr Organised. Suppose you'd have finished them a lot earlier if you hadn't had to move down south. You must have missed your weekends in the hills."

As usual, conversation meant they had covered distance and height without thinking about it, like that worrying thing when you realise you've been driving for a while but don't remember actually steering or changing gear. They were now on a series of false summits, easy enough going, and they slowed to allow the group to close up again. Chat and chocolate sustained them over the next twenty minutes until the summit cairn was first in sight then reached. With an awkward sense of ceremony the rest of the group stood back to let Gregor walk up to the cairn, stop for a moment, then add another stone to it. Cheering and whooping warmed the chill air then rucksacks were opened to bring out whisky, cheap sparkling wine, and cake.

Next came the photographs. First the big group, with Les leaving his camera on time exposure then just making it back as he slipped and nearly fell, to the delight of the rest. Then Gregor, displaying the half-smile of the older Scottish man. Finally a series of small groups with Gregor dragged in.

"Hey, cheer up and give us a smile!" shouted Cameron.

"Yeah, just think, you don't have to do this ever again," added Alex.

"He's thinkin' about all those Corbetts he has to do now," said Cameron.

"The ones wi' no paths."

Eventually the high-level party broke up and the descent was made. The minibus was refilled and made its way to the nearest pub, where the celebrations continued. They were not so much now celebrations of Gregor's last Munro: by now they were just the exuberant reactions to a good day on the hill, the loosening of tongues brought on by alcohol and the beneficial effects of outdoor exercise on mood. But mostly the alcohol. Three pints in and Gregor thought of himself as nothing but a Munroist. The 'hill of the sword' which had hung over him like a sword of Damocles had for the moment been dismissed as a problem. Of course he'd done it. Of course he had. Anyway, he'd done loads of them twice and thrice over, so stuff it. Next round.

Then he saw Sarah approaching him, looking a little embarrassed.

"Mr McKay – I mean Gregor, she began. "I'm sorry what I said about Munros and people cheating and stuff. My Mum says my tongue's my worst enemy. I think it's great, you climbing all those mountains."

"No problem, Sarah. Don't you worry yourself. Did your Grandad tell you to speak to me?"

"No, honestly. I just saw how happy everybody was and I felt guilty. And I don't like that feeling. Anyway, well done."

A week later Gregor McKay was filling up the car for a long journey. His rucksack was packed, and clothes for an overnight stay. His Munro book was open on the passenger seat at page 201. The next day he was back down the road, singing along to the CD blasting out *Runrig* songs.

"Fuck off Beinn a' Chlaidheimh, got you that time," he thought to himself. "Map, GPS, eyesight – all confirmed."

Two days later he got a phone call from Les.

"Hi Gregor, how y' doin'? Seen the news on the Scottish Mountaineering Club website? Another Munro re-classified. Beinn a' Chlaidheimh[6]. Mind it used to be a Corbett then they made it a Munro in our time. Now it's a Corbett again. Pity you had to do it all those years ago, eh?"

---

[6] Beinn a' Chlaidheimh began as a Corbett, a hill between 2,500 and 3,000 feet. In 1974 it was re-measured as just over the magic 3,000 feet. In the summer of 2011 a visit from a 'heighting' team from the Munro Society used improved GPS equipment to change its status back to that of a Corbett.

ABOUT THE AUTHOR

Alan Laing is a former English teacher who lives near Perth. He has written short plays for young people which have been performed in a dozen countries. In the last four years he has won three awards from Mountaineering Scotland for his fictional stories involving walking, climbing and mountains, as well as one award for poetry. He also provides lyrics for Perth's Jambouree Choir.

Climbing and walking has been a lifelong hobby of his, pursued with friends, with Duke of Edinburgh groups, and with his current employer – a West Highland Terrier. Having climbed most of the Munros he has recently branched out into long-distance trekking in the Italian Dolomites. His enjoyment of writing and walking have now combined to produce this anthology.

❖

THE PUBLISHER

Tippermuir Books Ltd (*est.* 2009) is an independent publishing company based in Perth, Scotland.

OTHER TITLES FROM TIPPERMUIR BOOKS

Spanish Thermopylae (Paul S. Philippou, 2009)

Battleground Perthshire
(Paul S. Philippou & Robert A. Hands, 2009)

Perth: Street by Street
(Paul S. Philippou & Roben Antoniewicz, 2012)

Born in Perthshire
(Paul S. Philippou & Robert A. Hands, 2012)

In Spain with Orwell (Christopher Hall, 2013)

Trust (Ajay Close, 2014)

Perth: As Others Saw Us (Donald Paton, 2014)

Love All (Dorothy L. Sayers, 2015)

A Chocolate Soldier (David W. Millar, 2016)

The Early Photographers of Perthshire
(Roben Antoniewicz & Paul S. Philippou, 2016)

Taking Detective Novels Seriously:
The Collected Crime Reviews of Dorothy L. Sayers
(Dorothy L. Sayers and Martin Edwards, 2017)

FORTHCOMING

Not So Fair a City: Dark Stories from Perth's Past
(Gary Knight, 2017)

*Wee Stories from the Crescent:
A Reminiscence of Perth's Hunter Crescent*
(Anthony Camilleri, 2017)

The Fair Maid of Perth: the Perth Edition
(Walter Scott, 2017)

The Tale o the Wee Mowdie
(Werner Holzwarth and Wolf Erlbruch, 2017)

All titles are available from
bookshops and online booksellers.

They can also be purchased directly at
www.tippermuirbooks.co.uk.
Tippermuir Books Ltd can be contacted at
mail@tippermuirbooks.co.uk